COASTAL CURSE

COASTAL ADVENTURES SERIES 8

DON RICH

Library of Congress PCN Data

Rich, Don

Coastal Curse/Don Rich

Florida Refugee Press LLC

Cover by: Cover2Book.com

Published by FLORIDA REFUGEE PRESS, LLC, 2021

Crozet, VA

PROLOGUE

I t wasn't the best book he had ever written, but even being less than his best meant it was still great. In her mind everything he wrote, everything he did, everything about him was great, and she could never get enough of him. Not that she'd ever *had* him, at least in the biblical sense. But that day was coming, and she was sure it wasn't too far off. She'd already met him in person twice, at book signings. And the second time he had recognized her, she was certain of it. The way he smiled at her, well, almost smiled. He wasn't much in the smiling department, he looked so serious all the time. But that would change once he was with her. It was destined to be a life-changing event for them both.

Even before reading his latest eBook release, she was the first one to order the paperback *and* the hardcover in addition to it, she was sure of this. No one else was as dedicated a fan as she. No, wait, fan wasn't the right word, maybe... follower. No, that wasn't right either. That would imply a one-sided relationship, and theirs was anything but. Devotee. That was it! This conveyed how devoted she was to him, and to helping him with his career. Her help, up to this point, had consisted of talking him up with her friends. Well, not *real* friends. Other than her contacts on social media, she didn't have "friends" that she hung out with in person. But she did have over a thousand social media contacts and followers from all around the world, most of them in other countries. They all knew about him, thanks to her. And she intended on telling him about all that she'd done for him.

One problem with this plan was she didn't quite know how to get in contact with him. There was an email address on his website, in the "back matter" of his books, and his newsletter, but that was probably answered by someone else. Likely that it was hooked to one of those automatic reply things and would be what people who don't really *know* him used to try to reach him. No doubt he would give her his cell phone number and *personal* email address if he only knew she wanted to be able to reach him.

She had come to the Florida Keys to track him down since she knew he was from there. Islamorada, to be precise, which was where she was now, standing outside the fishing outfitter store he owned. Or, apparently used to own. When she'd arrived, in the store was a newly framed front page of the local paper on the wall. In it was a picture of him as he was handing over the keys to the business to his longtime store manager. The accompanying story told of how in appreciation of the woman's twenty years of working with him, last month Sanford Morgan had made her a great deal on the purchase. She had gone to work there straight out of high school and had never worked for anyone else. Now she would be her own boss.

It was so like him to do this, to reward the loyalty of those around him. This is why she was sure that he would see and appreciate her dedication to helping him advance his writing career. Though she questioned the depth of loyalty of the new store owner. She hadn't been able to get her to understand that she and Sanford were friends and that she just needed to know how to get in touch with him here. The twit had the nerve to refer to him as "Sandy" like it was okay for her to be that familiar. And then questioning her honesty, saying that if she was a friend of his she'd have known that picture was weeks old, and that he had left for the season over two weeks ago.

The twit wouldn't answer anything more about where he had gone or when he'd be back. Then she told her if she wasn't there to purchase something, she needed to leave. Being cautious about giving out Sanford's whereabouts was admirable since she was certain many undesirable people might want to track him down. But anyone with any brains could see that she wasn't one of those cretins.

So, he'd already left for the season. The post office box listed on his author's website used to be in Onancock, Virginia, but last fall it had been changed to one in Cape Charles, a small town several miles farther south on the Eastern Shore of the Chesapeake Bay. She knew from reading his interviews that he lived on a boat of some kind, she just didn't know which one or where it was docked. Or even the name of it for that matter. But she would, and soon.

Now it was time for a road trip, over a thousand miles of it. Up to Cape Charles. It sounded like such a quaint place, the kind of place where a bestselling author would want to go for the summer. She was sure she'd find him there, and that he'd want her to seek him out. There was no way she was going to disappoint him.

1
____

BREAKERS

Just beyond the surf break off Smith Island, Virginia, Michael "Murph" Murphy trolled along in the *LNZ II*, his somewhat older thirty-one-foot Contender center console boat. Named after his fiancée and business partner, Lindsay Davis, it was powered by twin 250-horsepower Yamaha engines. Not overpowered by any means, but enough that he still had plenty of power in reserve in case he needed it to get farther away from the breakers in a hurry.

"Fish on, Murph!" His fishing partner, Eddie "Rev" Jones, plucked the spinning rod from its holder on the gunwale as line screamed off the spool. "This one's a hoss!"

Murph slowed the boat slightly, now splitting this time between watching the water ahead as well as the remaining rod, which was on his side of the boat. Suddenly that rod tip bent far over, and line began screaming off its reel. Murph grabbed it and started fighting this fish, which also felt like a substantial one. Now he was doing double duty, running the boat while simultaneously fighting his fish. Rev gave him a worried side glance.

On a flat calm day, this would be a piece of cake, but today was anything but calm. The six- to eight-foot swells they were battling were cresting and breaking just inside their location. Murph now started turning the bow out into the face of the oncoming swells. These breaking waves were what was churning the water behind them, mixing it with sand and sediment and turning it a murky blue-green color. Baitfish were swimming in small schools through this murk, enticing the larger bluefish to chase them into the cloudy water. It was this larger species the two men had targeted, to be smoked and combined with another species in the most unbelievable fish dip on the planet. They had been dragging their lures in the clearer water just outside of the surf where the larger fish were more likely to see them.

The two had been fighting to keep their footing in the rocking boat until the bow slowly turned, pointing up into the swells. Finally, they no longer had to lean against anything to stay upright. It was a good thing since as both fish got closer to the boat, they had to switch sides twice to keep their lines from crossing. If that happened, they would run the risk of one or both lines breaking from the friction if they rubbed together.

Three minutes later, the first of the razor-toothed creatures came over the side, followed a minute later by the second. It was a scenario they would repeat a few more times over the next hour or so until there were a half dozen nice-sized blues on ice in the fish box.

"All right, we have all the bluefish we need now, so on to the next ingredient," Murph said.

"This stuff is that good to go to all this trouble?"

"Trust me, Rev, it's like seafood crack. One spoonful and you're hooked. Sandy loves it, so this is going to be his 'welcome home' gift. But now we need some mackerel to round out the protein portion of the recipe. Baloney said he's already seeing them in the lower Chesapeake, and it should be a lot calmer in there."

"Anything beats this washing machine out here today, Murph. Being this close to those breakers makes me nervous."

"Yeah, I've gotten caught inside a rogue one before that broke farther out, and that's no fun," Murph said.

Rev was a former waterman turned preacher, and over the years he had been in his share of perilous situations out on the water. His admitting to being this nervous just punctuated the danger of fishing so near the breakers. Murph slowly pushed the throttles forward, bringing the boat up to a low cruising speed while making a wide, sweeping turn. Then he set a course that would take them out and away from the "business end" of the waves.

Paralleling the coast and running almost broadside to the swells made for a comfortable ride. They gently quartered each wave, cresting the tops and riding slightly sideways down the backs into the troughs that lay in between. When they finally cleared the bottom of the peninsula and made their turn toward Fisherman Inlet Bridge at the base of the bay, the swells became much smaller and closer together. Murph added more throttle and *LNZ II* now glided from crest to crest without dipping her bow down into the troughs.

As they passed *Mallard Cove Marina*, Murph scanned the two bars and grills next to the beach. He noted that each had a decent-looking lunch crowd for this early in the season, especially for midweek. He and Lindsay were the majority owners of the complex, and it was nice to be reassured that everything can run smoothly without his having to be around. He turned and looked back over the bow again, focusing now on the channel and the point where it passed under the bridge between the two wooden "fender" piers. Time to concentrate; hitting one of those could wreck your whole day.

SANFORD "SANDY" Morgan smiled from up on the flying bridge of his fifty-five-foot trawler, *Epilogue*. He looked over at his new buddy from Ocracoke Island, KC Shaw, who was curled up and asleep on the built-in bench seat on the side of the open-air flybridge. KC is no ordinary islander, he's about sixteen inches high, yet that's tall enough for him to be nicknamed "Stretch." He's an Ocracat, one of the feral cats which are born each year on Ocracoke, the southern-most inhabited island on North Carolina's Outer Banks. His dark gray and black tabby-marked fur gleamed in the sun, keeping him warm in the cool, early morning air.

Epilogue was at her cruising speed on the Elizabeth River in Virginia, on the Intracoastal Waterway. They had spent last night in a marina just beyond the river's northernmost lock. If everything went as planned today, they would reach *Casey's Cove* on the southern end of the Eastern Shore of Virginia, or as the locals call it, ESVA, a little after lunchtime. Right now, this portion of the river wasn't crowded, and they were making good time. But in an hour or so, the shores would no longer be lined with woods and green space, replaced instead by industrial zones loaded with everything from road salt and fuel depots to marine construction and salvage yards. Large interstate highway bridges passing overhead would mark *Epilogue's* entry into the congested urban areas of Chesapeake, Portsmouth, and Norfolk. By then, their speed would be reduced to a fast idle, especially in the vicinity of Naval Station Norfolk in Hampton Roads. The Navy got "touchy" about boats going fast near their aircraft carriers and the other vessels of Fleet Forces Command. But once they passed over the Hampton Roads Bridge-Tunnel on the Chesapeake Bay's southern boundary, they would again be free to throttle back up. So long as there weren't any naval vessels out and about, that was.

"Here you go, Sandy." His niece and crew member, Micah Monroe, came up the steps to the flybridge, a canvas bag slung over one arm. She reached in and pulled out a couple of travel mugs of coffee and a foil-wrapped pair of breakfast burritos she'd made down in the galley. Next came a can of cat food and a small dish that she filled and placed on the deck.

"See? I didn't forget you, KC."

The cat hopped down and sniffed the food before glaring up at her. He sniffed the food again and reluctantly began nibbling at it.

"You'll like your new home, KC. Plenty of fresh fish gets brought in there, so you'll get your fill again. Much better than that junk your pal here feeds you," Sandy said.

"And you've turned him into a beggar, Sandy. Nobody can bring a fish into the docks anymore without him showing up at the cleaning table," Micah scolded him.

Sandy frowned, "An island-dwelling descendant of Blackbeard's cats shouldn't be living off crap in a can."

Micah took the navigator's seat next to him as she shook her head, "He doesn't live on an island anymore, ESVA is a peninsula. And you don't know for sure that he's descended from Blackbeard's cats. Plus, this stuff gives him a properly balanced diet."

"Well, I don't know that he's not. And you can take the cat off the island, but you can't take the island out of the cat. Besides, the Chesapeake and Delaware Canal cuts the Eastern Shore off from the mainland, and the only way to get there is across a bridge, by boat, or by air. So, in my book that makes it an island. And fresh seafood *is* a big part of his properly balanced diet. That canned stuff smells like crap."

Micah rolled her eyes as she picked up her burrito. Once her uncle was dug in on something, there was no point in trying to argue with him.

In KC's case, Sandy did have some facts he could hang his hat on. Ocracoke Island has a rich and storied history. A big part of it is that back in the early 1700s it was a favorite anchorage for a man named Edward Teach and some of his friends. Teach, of course, was better known as Blackbeard the pirate, and ironically, this would also be the place where he would meet his end. But one of Blackbeard's early quartermasters had turned away from pirating by then, accepting a pardon from the North Carolina governor and using his share of the plunder to become a successful businessman. He later purchased Ocracoke, where some of his descendants still live to this day.

Legend says that these island folks aren't the only ones descended from someone who arrived with Teach. Blackbeard also brought with him a pair of cats, Chester and Anne (the latter named after his pirate friend, Anne Bonney) which he kept aboard his ship for rodent control. At least they were aboard until Teach met his end, his decapitated body thrown overboard. The Virginia mercenaries who killed the pirate also threw Teach's cats over the side. Teach's head was then brought back to Hampton, Virginia. There it was placed on a pike at the harbor entrance by order of the governor, who intended it as a gruesome reminder to all other pirates.

Teach's two cats managed to make it to shore where they quickly adapted to life in the marsh; it was either that or starve. They were soon joined by other cats whose ships visited the island in search of Blackbeard's legendary treasure, reputed to have been buried somewhere out on Springer's Point.

Nature harshly moderated the cat population through the limited availability of food and fresh water. Flooding from wash-over during hurricanes also periodically thinned the now nativized feline colony. As humans began permanently settling on the island, the waste from the emerging fishing industry became a new source of food for the colony, and it started to overexpand. But conditions in the marsh didn't improve with the growing population. Many of its members suffered, especially in the winter season with less to eat as well as its often wet, freezing, and extremely miserable conditions.

In the late 1900s group of Ocracokers banded together, determined to help nature control the population of the colony and improve the lives of its members. The group, led by a woman named Rita, established a volunteer program to trap adult cats. They were then spayed or neutered and released back into the wild. Each spring the new litters of kittens from the yet-to-be spayed cats are rounded up, and indoor homes are found for each of them, both on and off the island. These volunteers placed small shelters in the marsh, giving the colony members dry places to stay during periods of wet weather.

Sandy's good friend, Casey Shaw, met Rita a few years ago and learned about the organization, named Ocracats. Just before Sandy left on his trip back south for the winter, Casey told him about the island and its history, briefly mentioning the cats and the group's work. It was like giving free drugs to a junkie, as Sandy's writer instinct kicked in. Always on the lookout for new stories and character material, Ocracoke was put on Sandy's itinerary. But even he couldn't imagine what was about to happen after he tied up his boat at the small village.

He arrived on a slow midweek afternoon, then met Rita at her store and introduced himself. With no customers around, the two went outside and sat on the store's covered front deck while they talked. Since the subject was Ocracats, Sandy paid little notice as a year-old cat hopped up in his lap. He absentmindedly petted the cat, who began purring loudly. Rita was astonished.

Sandy asked, "What's wrong?"

"You're petting a cat that can't be petted."

Alarmed, he started to withdraw his hand and was instantly swatted by a paw, though without any extended claws. He hadn't been permitted to stop.

Rita said, "No, I mean he never lets anyone pet him. He ignores everybody, and when they try to pet him, they usually get clawed, bitten, or both. That, or he runs away. This is amazing."

"*This* cat? He's a sweetheart."

"You're quite a cat person."

He shook his head. "Not really. I mostly tolerate animals, and they do the same in return." He continued petting the cat.

"Maybe you just never met the *right* cat. Like him. He's never met the *right* human before. We tried adopting him out when he was little, but he was still way too wild for that. Two of our best foster families gave up and brought him back, so we had no choice but to turn him out here by the store. He sticks around, picking up meals on the side porch along with the others. He hasn't shown any interest in going back into the marsh where he was born. Mostly he hangs out under and around the porch, which is better than the marsh, but still not an ideal situation."

The cat now curled up in Sandy's lap, still purring but closing his eyes. "Well, great. Maybe now someone can adopt him."

Rita smiled, "Maybe someone already has."

"Who, me? No way, I live on a boat. Not exactly a great cat environment either. And like I said, I just tolerate animals." Sandy was now scratching the cat under his chin, and both looked quite content.

"Cats have been living on boats for hundreds of years, Sandy. Many crews consider them good luck." She told him the story of Chester and Anne.

"Good luck, eh? Tell that to Teach and his crew."

"Well, it's probably a moot point anyway, Sandy. This one's as independent as they get, and that's saying a lot."

Sandy studied the cat, who opened one eye and returned the look. "That marsh must be a nightmare for cats."

Rita replied, "If it was a healthy environment, we wouldn't work so hard to get them out of there. Usually, once they get beyond the kitten stage, there's no sense in trying to get them adopted. They're almost always too wild to domesticate by that point. We have them spayed or neutered and let them go. You can tell at a distance which ones have been 'fixed' by that notch in the ear that's done while they're still under anesthesia."

Sandy ran his finger over the cat's ear where a "V" shaped piece about a quarter of an inch had been removed. "I thought maybe this was from a fight."

"Nope, though Larry put up quite a fight when we caught him."

"Yeah, well, I'd put up a fight too before I'd let anyone cut off my... well, before I'd let anybody notch my ear and do everything else that comes with it." He looked down into the cat's eyes, which were now both open. "You don't look like a 'Larry.' Not a Moe or a Curly, either. More like a KC, for the guy that sent me here." The cat gazed back in silent agreement.

The two humans continued chatting for another fifteen minutes, while Larry/KC continued to be pampered. Finally, it was time for Rita to close her shop and put food out on the porch for the feline colony before she headed home. Sandy picked up the cat and placed him down on the deck as Rita shook her head.

"Nobody has ever been able to handle him like that without losing a quart of blood."

"Apparently, we have reached a level of understanding," Sandy said.

"Looks that way, Sandy."

"Well, nice to meet you. I love what you're doing here. Nice to see people getting together to do good things for animals."

She chuckled, "I thought you said you only tolerated animals." She knew that if this had been the case, he'd have never stopped by in the first place. Whether he wanted to admit it or not, he was a natural-born cat person.

"Mostly. Though there are always exceptions to rules." He looked down at KC, who was now rubbing against his leg. "Take care of yourself, KC."

Rita watched as Sandy went down the front ramp with the cat formerly known as Larry in hot pursuit, right on his heels. She called out, "The Village Variety Store has a great pet food and supply section, just in case you change your mind about adopting him." Not like you have a choice, she thought to herself. Over all of her years of being involved with Ocracats, what happened this afternoon was the strangest thing she'd ever seen. But she had learned early on that there are things that are just meant to be, and the pairing of these two was one of them. Somehow, she knew it wouldn't be the last she'd see of either of them.

2 HOME

Several hours later Micah brought tuna sandwiches up to the flybridge as they passed the last Navy ship docked at its pier. Sandy dug out some of the larger pieces of tuna from his sandwich and fed them to KC.

"Honestly, Sandy, you have ruined that cat."

"Yeah, well, he deserves some pampering after the way he had to start life."

"Pampering? He's had fresh Mahi, tuna, and snapper all summer long back in the Keys. He ate better than most of the tourists."

"Muse's pay. I've never written as fast or as well as I did this summer while he was right there with me. Seemed to have inspired you as well."

Micah was an up-and-coming independent author. A few years ago, her aunt had died, leaving Sandy alone and heartbroken. He sold his home in Islamorada, moving aboard *Epilogue*, determined to cruise up and down the east coast by himself, much to his two sisters' horror. Each then talked one of their daughters into crewing with Sandy that first year so he wouldn't be alone. They also worried about the "Widows with Casseroles Brigade" that had queued up to take their best shot at the well-known and very well-off recent widower. They both knew that in the short term, Sandy might be vulnerable to the wrong person. The plan was that the girls could act as "gatekeepers" for a while, making sure Sandy wasn't taken advantage of.

Since Micah and her cousin Carol were both aspiring writers, Sandy agreed to teach them the craft as part of their arrangement. One stipulation was that they had to agree to drop the "Uncle" from his name. He figured that his appearing to have two beautiful girlfriends in their twenties might make him look as dashing as some of his characters. And his sisters had figured correctly, as all but the most determined and scheming suitors quickly lost interest in this "new, wilder Sandy." His nieces easily handled the rest. Sandy's sisters knew their brother was now in good hands, and he quickly capitalized on his new reputation. In the waterfront bars along their route, the trio became recipients of round after round of free drinks from his fans who now saw him as a sort of literary Hugh Heffner.

Then, on his first cruise north, Sandy discovered the newly renovated *Bayside Resort and Marina* on ESVA. He became friends with its owner, the namesake of his feline friend. At that point, *Bayside* became his designated summer layover. But by his second season though the crowd had started to change, as the place became a popular getaway for the Washington, DC, elite. That wasn't a group Sandy was very comfortable with, and he started thinking about a change of scenery. Ironically, by that time Casey Shaw became a victim of his success, losing much of his privacy at *Bayside*.

Then in one of those stories for another day, circumstances beyond his control forced Casey to move. He purchased some property next door to *Mallard Cove Marina* down at the southern tip of ESVA, where he and his wife Dawn were also partners with Murph and Lindsay. This new twenty-one-acre property had a small, deepwater, natural cove that was large enough for his 110-foot Hargrave yacht which served as the floating home to both Dawn and himself. They built a few extra slips which now held the boats and houseboats of a handful of his closest liveaboard friends, including Sandy.

He was now down to just Micah as his crew. Carol had met her soulmate on ESVA, a young entrepreneur named Tyler MacKenzie. Carol shelved her writing aspirations to help Tyler run a charitable camp on ESVA for wounded warriors.

With *Epilogue's* move down to what has been dubbed *"Casey's Cove,"* Sandy discovered the perfect new lifestyle for himself, and now intended on leaving *Epilogue* there year-round. Today was the last leg of their final roundtrip to Florida. From now on, he'd fly back and forth whenever he wanted to visit his sisters.

As they passed through the channel over the Hampton Roads Bridge Tunnel, KC suddenly became animated, standing up on his bench seat. He stared off in the direction of Fort Monroe as his back arched and the fur along his spine stood on end. He hissed and growled, then relaxed a minute later and returned to his prior position.

Micah asked, "What the heck was up with KC?"

Sandy said, "I've never seen him do *that* before. But I did tell you he was from the line of Blackbeard's cats."

"So?"

"He was staring at the point where they displayed Teach's head on that staff."

"Very funny." She looked grossed out.

Sandy shrugged his shoulders. "I'm just saying... cats know things."

She gave him a sideways glance as she shook her head slowly, at her uncle's apparent lapse of sanity. Then KC opened one eye, looked at her, and grinned as if to say yes, cats know things, and yes, we can grin. Sandy didn't truly believe that KC's strange behavior was in any way connected to some supernatural or otherworldly event; he just wanted to tease his niece. Kind of the nautical equivalent of telling ghost stories around a campfire. But he thought to himself that was indeed some very strange behavior.

Sandy and Micah had purposely chosen to make this run in the shelter of the Intracoastal these past few days instead of out on the ocean. Had they run "outside" instead, they wouldn't have passed this way and would have missed out on seeing KC's strange act. But a steady onshore wind over the past few days had kicked up swells all along the mid-Atlantic coast, the same swells that Murph and Rev had battled this morning. Many of North Carolina's inlets on the Outer Banks were treacherous enough on the calmest of days, with sandy shoals that could quickly change locations within hours. The Intracoastal was a slower, but much safer alternative on rough days like today when a mechanical issue could force you to have to head in through one of these dangerous and unfamiliar inlets.

Now that they were entering the Chesapeake, Sandy set a direct course to Fisherman Inlet Bridge at the base of ESVA. Halfway across the almost twenty miles of water between Hampton Roads and Fisherman Island, Sandy spotted a familiar blue-green hulled sport fisherman. He switched his VHF radio over to the local fishing frequency.

"Hey, Gilligan! Are you torturing another poor charter with those cheap-assed cigars of yours or what?"

The reply was swift and loud, "I told you to quit callin' me that, you hack! Is that you comin' up from the south?"

"Roger that, I'm baaaack! If I recall correctly, you owe me some beer, and I'm here to collect."

"I'll take care ah that a little later. I had 'em lay in a big stock for ya at *Casey's Cove.* Just a few more hours left to go out here, then I'll be in ta drink some of it with ya."

"Good deal, Gilligan, because I'm fresh out. So, I'll meet you there."

"Good, see ya in there inna while. *My Mahi,* clear and standin' by."

"Gilligan" was none other than Captain Bill "Baloney" Cooper. He was a very colorful character who owned the two charter boats which comprised the "Dolphin Fleet," the *Golden Dolphin,* and *My Mahi.* The latter was what Bill was running today, which also served as the floating home of both his wife, Betty and him.

A New Jersey transplant with the accent to prove it, Baloney was now also the highest-paid cast member of the hit cable show, *Tuna Hunters,* which filmed here in the winter. But despite his now low seven-figure income, he remained the biggest beer mooch at *Mallard Cove,* with Sandy coming in as a close second.

Becoming such a big success hadn't affected Bill's choice of cigars, either; he still bought the cheapest ones available. Which was why Betty made the rule that he wasn't allowed to light up except out on the water, and even then only when he was well beyond the marina's breakwater. The rest of the time he kept an unlit "stick" in his mouth, except when he was drinking someone else's beer. And he was always drinking on someone else's tab, which was why Sandy was now confused. He'd never known Bill to be generous with any beer unless it didn't belong to him. There had to be more to this story, and he figured he'd get answers at some point later today.

After ten more miles, *Epilogue* passed under *Fisherman Inlet Bridge.* Ahead on the left was *Mallard Cove's* beach, with the thatched-roofed *Driftwood Stage* out in front and to the side of the *Cove Beach Bar.* A handful of red, twin-hulled rental ESVACats were up on the beach next door to the *Catamaran Bar and Grill.* A landscape crew with a skid loader was in the process of installing some tall, cold-hardy palms high on the beach next to both bars.

"Wow! Check out the new tropical look. Really feels like home now, doesn't it, Sandy?"

"Well, the Keys don't feel like home anymore with all those damned new people, so this'll have to do. Those aren't exactly coconut palms, but they're close enough. I have a feeling it will be even more like home to you though when you see Jeff."

Micah smiled, since Sandy's comment was dead-on. Jeff Smith was the captain of Casey and Dawn's fifty-five-foot Jarrett Bay sport fisherman, *Predator.* For the past year and a half, the two had been an "item," enough of one that Jeff had flown down to Islamorada three times this past winter to see her. They were both happy about Sandy's plan to keep *Epilogue* here year-round.

They were approaching the riprap jetties which protected the inlet to *Mallard Cove Marina's* protected basin. Sandy had to slow to yield the right of way to a large yacht that was towing a large center console outboard behind it. The yacht was in *Smith Island Inlet Chan-*

nel, approaching from Sandy's starboard side, headed straight in for *Mallard Cove Marina.* There was something vaguely familiar about the larger boat, but he couldn't place it at first. The huge eighty-six-foot hull had faux longitudinal seams, designed to make it look like it was wood-planked, even though the entire boat was made of fiberglass. He finally recognized it as an Outer Reef, a well-known luxury yacht brand. This one had a wide blue waterline and an even wider matching stripe that ran fore and aft just under the sheer line.

"That looks like the boat that woman Betsy owns. You know, the one we met back in Palm Beach."

Micah nodded, "Betsy Riggins. And you're right, it does." As the boat continued past, allowing them to see the name, *Cheri,* and the hailing port of *Palm Beach,* Micah continued. "That's hers all right. I wonder what it's doing here?"

"Maybe making a fuel stop before pushing on up north? She seemed pretty interested in hearing about this place though at that damn party."

Micah laughed, "She seemed more interested in hearing about you than *Mallard Cove.* And she seemed nice."

"About the only nice thing about that party. And yes, she *was* nice."

An old fishing client and friend from back before the days of his success as a writer had insisted that they stop over in Palm Beach as they passed through. Sandy hadn't realized the man and his wife intended on throwing a cocktail party in his honor. That's just how things were there, even at the tail end of the social season. If you had a celebrity friend, whenever possible you showed them off on the cocktail circuit. It was part of how all the unofficial social standing points for each season get tallied. In Palm Beach, "bagging" a best-selling author who tried to keep as low of a profile as Sandy did was considered quite the coup. No doubt the party had been talked about for days, even after *Epilogue* was well beyond Florida's territorial waters. Sandy was glad that was the last time he'd be cruising through there. After that ambush, as far as he was concerned, Palm Beach was now relegated to his list of "fly-over territory."

Though he had been slightly distracted after seeing the yacht and being reminded of the woman, he quickly refocused on the task at hand. Straight ahead, just past the marina's jetties, was the start of the Virginia Inside Passage. This protected portion of it was almost two miles long—a deep but narrow channel dredged diagonally through the very tip of ESVA.

But Sandy and Micah wouldn't be going that far down the channel. Several hundred yards ahead on the left was a cut that led through the narrow strip of land which enclosed *Casey's Cove*. Getting his fifty-five-foot trawler safely through the inlet opening was a big enough challenge for Sandy. He marveled at the skill of Casey's captain, Frank Cunningham, who threaded this needle with *Lady Dawn*, a deeper drawing vessel exactly twice the length and almost twice the width of *Epilogue*.

Micah was now down on the bow, getting the dock lines ready as Sandy made his turn at idle speed, using his bow thruster to tighten the turn's radius. The change in speed and the noise of the thruster alerted the cat that something important was happening, so KC stood up and stretched. He scanned the area around the cove as they entered. Sandy pulled straight into their slip on the floating dock and tied up to the finger pier. Then things got interesting when the dock boxes and the dock freezer were then unloaded. The cat knew those hadn't moved from the deck since they left Islamorada.

"Hello, Sandy! Hey, Micah!" Casey Shaw was walking down the main dock from the far end where *Lady Dawn* was berthed. Jeff Smith was a few steps behind him.

"Hello, yourself. Did you two time this on purpose so you didn't have to help lug these heavy son-of-a-bitches off the boat?" He indicated the dock boxes.

Casey laughed. He'd have been disappointed if Sandy hadn't replied with some sarcastic comment, his usual way of doing things. "I missed you too, Sandy."

"Well, I hope it was enough so that you remembered to have some cold beer on hand."

"I figured that you might be 'fresh out' when you got here. All taken care of, Sandy." He pointed to a golf cart that was approaching from the *Cove*. Its flatbed was loaded with two cases of Jamaican Red Stripe beer. "This should be enough to get you through until you can get to the store for more."

"Ah, you're a good man, Casey Shaw! Wait, is any of that cold?"

"No, but we laid in a stock of it on ice up at C2. The gang has a welcome home shindig planned for you later today."

C2 stood for the *Cove Club*, a facility Casey and Dawn built next to *Casey's Cove*. It included a clubhouse with a pool table, bar, steam room, and loft guestroom. Outside was a heated pool and hot tub with a large stone deck, a covered outdoor kitchen, and a round stone fire pit. One heck of a great place for a party. And unlike the cocktail nightmare he had attended in Florida, gatherings with the gang here were unpretentious, laid back, fun, and welcome.

"Great! Now, you can give me a hand getting these cases aboard and into the fridge before we go up and get into those cold ones. Gilligan has already claimed the credit for them, and I want to get there before he also tries taking ownership. And it's not like those two are going to be a help to anybody for the rest of the afternoon." He motioned at Jeff and Micah who were now standing on the main dock, lost in their own world together.

With no room in the galley for so much beer, they stacked the cases neatly on the aft deck, putting a dozen bottles in the outside bar fridge. They had just finished when KC hopped up on Sandy's outdoor writing desk. He stared intently into the eyes of his name-sake as if performing a "Vulcan mind probe."

Casey said, "So this must be who I saw a glimpse of on that video call a while back. You have a boat cat now." It was more of a question than a statement since Sandy hadn't seemed to Casey to be much of a pet person.

"It's not like I had a choice. I stopped by to talk to your friend Rita, and he followed me back to the boat."

"She's probably sworn out a warrant for you for cat abduction."

"Just the opposite. We stayed on Ocracoke an extra day, to make sure he had a chance to go back over to her shop. He stuck with the boat." Sandy went on to tell KC's full story. As he did, Casey reached over to pet the cat's head, only to be rebuked with a hard paw-slap to the top of his hand.

"Hey!"

"Did he use his claws?"

"No, but he's strong."

Sandy said, "If he didn't use his claws it means he likes you, he's just not ready for you to pet him yet. Give it time. People he doesn't like, he shreds their hands instantly like pizza cheese."

"How do you keep him from running off?"

"I don't, but he doesn't. He's decided that *Epilogue* is his home."

"Only because you're on it." Micah had come aboard with Jeff. "He adores Sandy and tolerates me. Though I can pet him now, thanks to a few pounds of grouper and snapper this summer."

Casey asked, "He likes raw fish?"

Micah nodded. "He likes fish, period. He'll eat it any way it gets offered to him and steal it if it isn't. That cat will claw your face off for a shrimp tail."

She no sooner finished saying that before the cat put his nose up in the air, sniffing something on the breeze that was wafting around the boatshed next door. He hopped down onto the deck and was over on the dock in a flash. He took off at a fast trot up the ramp and was quickly out of sight beyond the building.

"Is someone cooking fish over at C2?" she asked.

Casey nodded. "Murph and Rev have been smoking some blue-fish and mackerel this afternoon."

"Making 'Chesapeake Crack'?" Sandy looked hopeful. That was the nickname of the smoked fish spread that Casey and Murph made which was so fiercely addictive.

"It was supposed to be a surprise for you."

Sandy smiled, "I knew I liked those boys. But they're in for a surprise of their own if that fish isn't in the smoker or sealed up in a container." He'd no more finished speaking than they heard angry yelling coming from beyond the boatshed. He laughed, "It wasn't."

The four hurried over to C2 to find Murph with his hand in the sink of the outdoor kitchen, running water over a gouged and bleeding hand. Rev was holding a tray loaded with smoked fillets up in the air while KC circled him, eyeing the tray.

Murph said, "Watch out, that's a rabid cat! Damn thing attacked me!"

"He is NOT rabid; he had all his shots at Ocracats. And if you'd have only given him a taste of the fish, he'd have left you alone," Sandy told him.

"You KNOW that furry nightmare?" Murph was still mad.

"I should. We share quarters on my boat. Hi there, Rev. Mind if I lighten that just a bit?"

"Hey, Sandy, welcome back." He lowered the tray far enough for Sandy to break off a piece of a warm fillet, while still warily eyeing KC.

Sandy handed some of the smoked fish to Murph. "Here, feed him a small piece."

"Are you nuts? I'm not letting him get a shot at my other hand!"

"He won't hurt you if you're feeding him. Trust me."

"You, I trust. Your pet wildcat, not so much."

"You've faced down guys with guns! Don't tell me you're scared of a cat."

Murph reluctantly bent down and offered KC the fish, which was quickly taken out of his hand. He repeated it with a few more small pieces. When he stood back up, KC began licking his paws, having accepted that dinnertime was over. For now.

Sandy repeated the story he'd just told Casey as he passed some beers around from the cooler. "He'll find the cleaning table in no time. Just make sure to give him a little bit of whatever you're cutting up, and you won't get clawed. He's an island cat, and he loves his fish. Just give him a taste and you'll be friends."

Murph wrapped his wounded hand in paper towels. "I wish you had told me that before I learned the hard way."

Sandy shrugged. "Some hardheaded people learn better that way. You know, people like you."

The Haitian mambo known as Mama Cecile came out of the trance where she had been communicating with the Loa, an intermediary between Bondye and humanity. This time she had learned she was to repay a familial debt by saving a life that had saved another. It was a white man, a non-believer, who years ago had saved one of her own blood; one who might have perished if not for his kindness. Bondye had decreed this man and one of his own must, in turn, be saved. This was her task, and it must be done. The Loa had told her what she needed to do to accomplish it, and now she needed to pack since she had a long trek ahead from here in Miami to a place called *Mallard Cove*. But the distance did not matter; the debt must be repaid.

3 THE BIG ASK

Donna DuBois looked at her watch as she pumped her gas at the huge tourist trap a few hundred yards shy of the North Carolina state line. The anti-collision lights atop the tower with the giant sombrero hat winked on and off in the growing dusk. The amusement rides underneath it weren't operating yet since schools still had several more weeks to go before the summer break. Still, I-95 had been a crowded nightmare, loaded with slow-driving snowbirds headed for their northern destinations. A bunch of them were crammed into the slot machine casino just across the parking lot.

With many of the old snowbirds now starting to pull off for the night, she figured she had another five hours to go before she reached Richmond. Then two more on I-64, and half an hour across the Chesapeake Bay Bridge Tunnel. If everything went well, she'd hit the Eastern Shore sometime after two a.m. Then she'd find a hotel and make her way up to Cape Charles in the morning. She'd start looking through the local marinas there for Sanford's boat. He was going to be so surprised and delighted when he saw her; it was wonderful to have someone like her as devoted to him. Yes, tomorrow was going to be a big day for them both.

~

When Baloney arrived for the party, Sandy was sporting a silkscreened tee shirt with the caption: "I'm only here for the beer." Baloney broke out in a huge grin as soon as he saw it. "Now there's some truth in advertisin'! Wish I'd ah thought ah that one."

"I almost got one for you, but it would've been a waste of ink. Everybody knows you're a 'suds mooch,' Gilligan."

"Yeah, well, it takes one ta know one, you hack. Speakin' of which…"

Sandy pointed to a cooler over by the grill. "In there."

After retrieving a bottle for Betty and one for himself, Baloney said, "Well? Aren'tcha gonna thank me for the beer?"

"I heard that everybody pitched in, and they had to fight off a flock of moths when they finally got you to open your wallet."

"Funny guy. At least you can't say I never bought you a beer, ya moocher."

Sandy chuckled and held up his bottle. "That was what I missed the most this winter, Gilligan, drinking your beer."

Baloney grinned and clinked his bottle against Sandy's. "Likewise."

The flames in the fire pit provided the only illumination as the last remaining handful of the group sat around it, having their final beers of the night. The rest of the party attendees had started trickling back to their boats and houseboats over an hour ago.

As "welcome home" parties went, this one had been memorable. Everyone had been happy to see Sandy and Micah again and to hear their stories about their trip. Not quite sure yet of all the people in this new environment, KC had stuck close to Sandy, carefully watching each unknown person approach. He hadn't allowed any of the strangers to pet him except for Murph, who had been sneaking him tidbits of fish dip. Now as a recognized "fish provider," he was on the cat's approved person list.

KC was curled up in Sandy's lap, his eyes reflecting the flames in an eerie way. He seemed to be listening to all the stories that were being told. That, or he was evaluating those telling them. Maybe both.

Lindsay Davis was saying, "You know, Sandy, if I had to bet on what kind of animal you might've shown up with, my money would've been on a dog, not a cat."

"It's not like I had a choice, Lindsay."

She was one of Sandy's favorite people. A pretty blonde in her late twenties, Lindsay had lived with Murph for the past few years. She had been his fishing mate back when they chartered his vintage Rybovich sport fisherman, the *Irish Luck* before he traded up to his current rig, a sixty-foot Merritt. Back then they had lived aboard and followed the tournament circuit, a hard but rewarding life. A huge seven-figure win at one of the richest tournaments in the world then allowed them to purchase a very run-down *Mallard Cove Marina,* which Murph had intended on renovating over time. Lindsay was the one who talked him into allowing Casey, Dawn, and a handful of other partners to invest in it with them. Their new partners' access to a large pool of capital allowed for an accelerated buildout of the property. Casey and Dawn also brought in their management team from their company, McAlister and Shaw. They designed and supervised the creation of the successful complex that it was today. Lindsay's vision and determination were part of why Sandy liked her; she could also handle Murph's stubborn side during those times when he needed a good swift kick in the hindquarters. He was glad when the two had finally gotten engaged last year.

She replied, "With a pet, you always have a choice, Sandy."

He shook his head. "Not and leave him there outside all winter. I know he was better off than the cats who still live in the marsh, at least having that deck roof above him. But when he followed me back aboard, he wasn't skittish at all about coming into the cabin. We both know that like me, you wouldn't have had the heart to make him go back ashore, either."

"You're a good man, Sandy Morgan," Rev commented.

"Yeah, well, don't let that get around, it'll spoil my image," Sandy grunted.

Of all in the group, Rev was a relatively new person to Sandy. He'd met him shortly before he left for Florida, he was the pastor of the Watermen's Church of ESVA. Sandy had never been much of a churchgoer, his attendance had always been limited to the occasional funeral or wedding, and Rev knew better than to try to push Sandy into attending his services. Rev's congregation was comprised mostly of active and retired watermen and their families who weren't the kind of people who responded well to being pushed, either. But they did respond to Rev.

As a former waterman himself, Rev had been a hard drinker and brawler before hearing his calling. After that revelation, he had come to understand the difference between blind drunkenness and having a few beers, and how reasoning worked better than brawling. He discovered his talent for reading people and saw straight through Sandy's tough exterior. That was a façade he created for his tough writer's image. Well, at least part of it was a put-on.

"I wouldn't dream of 'outing' you, Sandy. But if people start finding out that you're a cat person..."

Sandy scowled, "What, are you taking lessons from Gilligan now? I am NOT a 'cat person.' I live in *Casey's Cove* because I don't want to be around a lot of people. This way my readers only see *what* I want them to *when* I want them to of me. And KC hangs around me because he's a good judge of character as well as being one badass cat."

Murph said, "Good judge of character? I had to super-glue those gouges on my hand to make them stop bleeding. You need to clip his claws!"

"Hence the badass part. He can take care of himself. And you never clip the claws of a cat who has access to the outdoors, so he can defend himself against other animals. Did you see when Tank went after him earlier? One set of needle-sharp claws on each side of his nose, and he learned fast to leave him be." Tank was Marlin and Kari Denton's large white Labrador retriever who had come with them to the party. They rounded out the list of residents of *Casey's Cove*. "Besides, you two get along fine now. Don't think I didn't see you giving him all that fish dip tonight and then finally being able to pet him. By the way, if he wakes me up in the middle of the night with a case of cat-gas from that stuff, I'm going to bring him over and lock him in your houseboat."

Murph said, "That wasn't Tank's fault, he thought his Uncle Sandy had brought him a new chew toy. Yeah, he learns fast, so there's no way he'll make that mistake again. And I don't need updates on your cat's gastric issues. What are you gonna do with him when you fly back to the Keys next winter?"

Sandy shook his head. "I'm not going back there for the winter. I'd rather watch the change of seasons here than go see the 'change of license tags' down there. When I go, it'll only be for short visits."

"What about your condo," Lindsay asked.

"Never bought one. I looked at a few, but none that I liked. Damned things were all 'concrete human filing cabinets' full of snowbirds. KC would need a litter box there, and I'm not living with one of those things. It's why I had a cat door installed in *Epilogue's* aft bulkhead so he can take care of business on his own. Besides, I realized that the kind of people who are moving in down there now aren't my idea of fun.

"You have no idea how much I've missed this, kicking back around a fire with you lunatics, and drinking your beer. It would've only been better if it had been Gilligan that bought all the brew. It's a shame he bugged out early, I wanted to keep abusing him." He chuckled and saw the smiles appear on their faces. If you didn't know the two of them very well, you might think they were really at odds.

"There *is* something about this place, isn't there? It has a pull of its own," Lindsay said.

Sandy shook his head. "It isn't just the place. As I said, it's the people. Without y'all, it would only be another piece of dirt and water on the edge of a swamp with a few pilings stuck into the muck. All y'all are what drew me back here. And if any of you tell Gilligan that, I'll sic my attack cat on you."

Donna woke up after getting a little over four hours of sleep and then slowly recalled where she was. It had been just before three a.m. when she finally checked into the *Mallard Cove Hotel*. This was the first hotel on ESVA, right at the end of the *Chesapeake Bay Bridge Tunnel*. Even in the dark, the long bridge potions of it reminded her of the Overseas Highway she'd taken down and back from the Keys.

She dressed quickly and then checked out, asking the clerk if there was a good breakfast place between here and Cape Charles. He recommended the *Cove Restaurant* across the parking lot but mentioned there was also a quaint coffee shop and café on the main street in Cape Charles. She opted for the latter since she wanted to get up there as soon as possible. Plus, she figured that maybe someone at the coffee shop might be able to tell her where to find Sanford's boat. Traffic was light as she drove out onto US 13 for the less than a half-hour drive to the scenic little town on the edge of the Chesapeake Bay.

"Glad we stuck with beer last night," Murph said as he and Lindsay approached Sandy's table at the *Cove Restaurant*.

Sandy motioned to a pair of empty chairs, "Always a good option, especially on a Thursday night. Though I used to hurt myself a bit on beer too, way 'back in the day.' Slowing up a bit on the hard stuff now."

Murph asked, "Writing today?"

He shook his head. "Giving myself an extended weekend off. Recuperating from that long haul back up here. Need to stock up on groceries and get settled in. I'll get back into my writing rhythm on Monday. But as part of that 'settling in,' you have no idea how much I've been looking forward to this morning's breakfast. There's no better place around."

Soon after their server took their orders, Micah came in. Sandy could see something was wrong even before she sat down. "Do I need to go punch Jeff in the nose?"

"Hmm? Oh, no, everything with us is fine." She still looked apprehensive.

"Okay, that's good." Still, he could see she wasn't happy. "Are you going to make me play twenty questions here or what?"

"No, Uncle Sandy. It's just that I need to ask you for a favor that I don't want to, but I still need to."

With her stumbling over words like that, Sandy knew this was going to be a big ask. Micah hardly ever slipped up and called him "Uncle" in public anymore. But she was one of his most favorite people in the world, and never asked for much.

"Whatever it is, the answer is yes," he said.

"Wait. You need to know what it is first." She grimaced and her brow furrowed.

"Not really. I'm happy to do whatever I can for you."

"You know that coastal readers and writers group cruise I'm going on in a week? I just got an email, Travis MacIntosh, the highly ranked New York News bestselling author who was set to lead the main discussion had to have an emergency appendectomy last night. There's no way he'll be well enough to attend the cruise. Without him holding the main discussion group, we're worried that there might be some cancellations or no-shows since he is such a huge draw. Don't get me wrong, all the *TropicalAuthors.com* authors and our scheduled guest writers are great, they're just not as well known yet. But like you, Travis is one of the top ten writers in the country. All those best-sellers and the movies; he sold a ton of cabins for us. And you know how this is all about us getting exposure to more readers."

"And now you need a replacement for him."

"Yes. We need someone as big or bigger of a draw to guarantee we don't lose attendees. And more of your books have been made into movies than just about any other contemporary writer. You would be an even bigger draw than he is."

Sandy sighed, holding up his hand with his palm out in a "stop" gesture. "As I said, I'll do it."

"Really? I know how much you hate public meet-and-greets and book signings." She looked concerned.

"They wouldn't be that bad if they didn't involve having to deal with all those people."

"But your readers love you!"

Sandy shook his head, "No, they like who they think I am, the person who they want me to be. They get me mixed up with my characters. I feel like I can't be who I truly am in public, or I'll offend somebody. Then it'll end up in the papers or on social media and I'll get an angry call from my publisher. She'll remind me about how much money their company has tied up in me, and how I need to mind my manners in public, that it's all in my contract, yada, yada, yada.

"So, it's easier for me to 'behave' when I'm harder to find. Which is why I love this place so much. For the most part, people don't recognize me around here nearly as often. And that bunch of lunatics from last night that I call my friends? I can say whatever I want without insulting them because they all know me. The *real* me." He paused a second then looked at Murph and Lindsay. "No offense meant with the 'lunatics' comment."

Lindsay smiled, "None taken. Coming from you, I take it as a compliment."

"See? That's what I meant about this place and all of you." He leaned back in his chair. "I don't have to worry about seeing something I've said being quoted in print the next day." He pointed to his copy of the local *ESVA Telegraph* on the table in front of him.

"Which is why I didn't want to ask you. I don't want you to be uncomfortable, Sandy. I want you to be able to relax and have fun now that we're back here," Micah said.

"I'll be okay, kid, don't worry. By the way, where are we going on this thing?"

"We start at Norfolk, then on to Bermuda, and back to Norfolk."

"Get me the best room that's available," Sandy asked.

"I've already arranged for us to take over the owner's suite that

Travis MacIntosh had booked. It has two bedrooms plus a living room and bar."

"A bar, eh? Things are looking up... wait a minute... you've already booked this? So, you knew beforehand I was going to agree to go? What happened to not wanting to even ask me?"

She blushed. "Well, I didn't want to. But if you hadn't agreed to do it, Travis was going to have to cancel the cabin anyway. So, I was just hedging my bets like you would have done."

"You'd have had to cancel it if you couldn't deliver me?"

Micah nodded. "Pretty much. I told them you probably wouldn't come, but that I'd ask anyway."

"Well, go tell them that I'll be there and that it's only because of you. And send an email to my publisher, I'm sure they'll want to put stuff on social media about it." He sighed.

"I'm sorry, Sandy."

He broke out in a grin as a thought dawned on him. "Don't be. It's in my contract that I have to do a certain number of personal appearances each year. Guess what kiddo, Norfolk, Bermuda, and on-board ship count as three! I won't have to do any more until fall. Oh, and make sure to send a few cases of hardcovers of my latest book over to the boat for the book signings."

"I've got it covered, Sandy. Then I'm going up to Cape Charles to pick up our mail."

"Good. And how about swinging by the grocery store for provisions on the way back?"

"Will do. See you in a few hours."

After Micah left, Lindsay said, "I thought you were going to get your groceries."

"No, I said we needed to lay in some groceries and then get settled in. I didn't say *who* was going to get the groceries and who was going to do the settling-in. This seemed like the best scenario for the proper division of labor." When Lindsay rolled her eyes he said, "Hey, I just saved her bacon with her friends. Now it's her turn to bring home the bacon, literally. Speaking of which, here comes more of it." Their server had arrived with his long-awaited *Cove* breakfast.

4 NEW FRIENDS

Murph and Lindsay left Sandy sitting at the table by himself after they finished breakfast. He was enjoying a leisurely third cup of coffee while engrossed in the *ESVA Telegraph*, catching up on the latest local happenings.

"Is this seat taken?"

Sandy looked up from his paper, irritated by the intrusion. But behind the chair across from him was a smiling Betsy Riggins, who was already in the process of sitting down. Even though she was sitting without an invitation, he was happy about this interruption. There was something about this woman that he had instantly found appealing when they met back in Palm Beach. Probably somewhat because she, like Sandy, was anything but timid. That, and the fact that she didn't stand there, waiting for him to jump up and give her a welcoming hug. In Palm Beach, that was the expected protocol even with acquaintances, not just friends. But here she wasn't trying to play by those rules. He liked that.

"Don't look so surprised, Sandy. After you described this place to me a week and a half ago, I told you that I was interested in seeing it." She signaled the server for a cup of coffee of her own.

"I know you did, but you certainly didn't let any grass grow under your feet. Just stopping by on your way up north?"

"Sandy, at our age time becomes increasingly more valuable. You can sit around, think about things, and miss out. Or you can do them by being a bit more impetuous. And no, I'm not on my way farther north, this was my destination. The way you described it was intriguing. I love the two beach bars, and this joint reminds me of the old *Sailfish Marina Galley Grill* from thirty years ago, an old post-fishing hangout of mine. You did a great job of capturing my interest, and not just about this place. I even read one of your books this week. Liked it well enough, but really liked your bio. Straight and to the point, without a lot of fluff and crap. Oh, thank you, dear," she said to the server who had brought her coffee. She sipped it without adding sugar or cream.

"I saw you coming in yesterday. I was just getting here myself."

She replied, "That was my crew. I flew up this morning. Had a few things to do back in Palm Beach before I left, so I sent them on ahead with the boats."

Mimi Carter, the general manager of food operations was approaching, making the rounds of the tables. When she spotted Betsy, her face lit up.

"Betsy! What are you doing here? It's so good to see you!"

This time Betsy got up and hugged Mimi, "Great to see you, kiddo! I didn't know you were in Virginia, too. I lost track of you after you left St. Thomas. That last one was a heck of a tournament!"

Sandy was surprised. "You've done some tournament fishing, Betsy?"

Mimi laughed, not waiting for Betsy to answer him. "Not just fished, but won and set a few records while she did. I thought you two knew each other, Sandy. You didn't know that you were having coffee with Betsy Janvier?"

"Betsy Janvier? I thought your last name was Riggins. I've been hearing about Betsy Janvier for years."

"Janvier was my late husband's name. After he died, I went back to using my maiden name."

Mimi said, "It's funny that two fishing legends are sitting together, not knowing who each other are."

"I know exactly who he is, Mimi. At least I thought I did. I had him checked out after we met a week ago." When Sandy looked surprised, she said, "What? A gal can't be too careful these days you know. Half the people you meet in Palm Beach, well, let's just say that appearances can be deceiving, and the reality doesn't match up with the hype. After Claude passed away, some of the less desirable ones came flooding in on the tide, not even having the decency to allow me space and time to grieve. And before you ask, he and your wife both passed within a month of each other, so you know how long that takes. Not that you're ever the same again, at least I'm not."

Mimi could see this was a conversation that the two of them needed to have without her around. "Well, are you here for a while, Bets? Maybe we can get together, have a drink and catch up."

"Absolutely, on both counts. My boat is at the end of the far dock. Drop on by whenever you want."

After Mimi resumed her table-hopping, Sandy said, "You're right. You're never the same. Life isn't the same. So, you adapt to the 'new normal' and you move on."

"And you've done a lot of moving on, Sandy?"

"Sold my house, moved aboard the boat, and tried to become a snowbird."

Betsy laughed, "You? A 'Keys Conch' trying to become a snowbird?"

"I know. I wasn't that good at it. I used to dock up at *Bayside*, a bit north of here on the bay. But it started getting overrun with DC types, so impressed with their jobs and themselves. Then the owners, Casey and Dawn Shaw, who I'd become friends with, decided to bug out and move down here on their boat. There's a bit more to the story, but we'll save it for another day.

"Anyway, I met the crazy bunch that was here after Micah and I brought *Epilogue* down. Then we made one last cruise to the Keys, and I handed my old shop over to the manager who's been with me forever. After we cast off, I never looked back. But you knew that part."

She nodded, "You gave me the abbreviated 'Cliff's Notes' version of it at the party. I didn't get any more than that since Micah was running interference for you. I thought you two were together until later our hosts told me she was your niece by blood and not a 'niece.' So much of that going on down there, older guys with younger women. And vice versa."

Sandy laughed. "I used to have two of my nieces on board with me. My two sisters' idea. They liked it because the image of me having two young live-in girlfriends ran a lot of the 'widows with casseroles brigade' away. Gals aren't the only ones who can't be too careful these days you know."

"Touché. And sorry, I left my casserole back in Florida, though we *are* the same age."

"Oh, I didn't mean..."

Betsy cracked up. "Don't worry, I love that phrase! First time I've heard it though. So, who is this 'crazy bunch' that you mentioned? Is Mimi part of it?"

"Mimi? Not directly, though she's on the edge of it. Stick around here long enough and you'll meet all of them. Most are partners in this place and a few other properties around the bay."

"Speaking of being around, where's your trawler, I didn't see her in here. Got her out of the water for maintenance?"

"That's right, you just got here and don't know your way around yet. She's hidden away in *Casey's Cove* next door. As I said, I was having privacy issues up at *Bayside*, and to a lesser degree when I got down here as well. Casey and Dawn Shaw are very private people. They bought the property next door that had the perfect little cove where they and some of their friends could dock in their own little complex."

"Complex?" She raised her eyebrows.

"Part of why I'm going to stay here year-round. But I'm getting ahead of myself. We meet at a party, and a week later you have your boat moved a thousand miles just so we can have coffee?"

"As I said, I have a new appreciation for the value of time. And I thought I felt a connection with you like we had a 'moment' at the party. Something that hadn't happened since I met Claude. I'm sorry if I read it wrong, but at least it brought me to this place, and the heck out of Palm Beach." She looked embarrassed.

"To tell you the truth, I felt there was something about you, too, that night. So, I'm glad you're here, I'm enjoying this."

Betsy looked relieved. "I am as well. And this coffee is so good it's almost worth the trip all by itself." They both laughed.

There were only two marinas attached to the harbor at Cape Charles, although a third was being built in front of a huge residential and commercial complex that was under construction. Neither of the dockmasters she talked to knew anything about Sanford Morgan's boat. That, or they were being very coy, protecting the great man. The only identifying characteristics of the boat that she'd seen had come from a picture on the back flap of his latest book's dust cover. Sanford was seated in front of a small desk with a laptop, which was obviously on an open aft deck. The problem was that none of the boats in either marina had an aft deck that matched the one in the background of the picture.

She was starting to get aggravated until she ran into a man tying up his sailboat who asked her to catch his stern line. Not certain about what to do with it, she hung onto the line until he came ashore and attached it to a dock cleat. Figuring he was now obliged to return a favor, she explained that she was there trying to find her friend's boat. While he thought it was weird that she didn't know the name, type, or even the length of the boat, he suggested she try the docks at the north harbor. It was on the other side of town, connected to a newer development.

Now discouraged after having driven over and back to that marina with the same negative result, she went to the coffee shop for a late breakfast of a bagel and coffee. After giving the server her order, she showed her Sanford's

picture, loudly emphasizing that she was a close friend of his and needed to find him. The woman truthfully told her that she'd never seen him in the shop, nor anywhere around Cape Charles, and she'd lived here her whole life. Then she moved over to a neighboring table where two young women were finishing their breakfast and one was staring at the other woman. The waitress subtly shook her head and tapped the side of her forehead to signal that the woman seemed to be "a tad off." Then she warmed their coffees before moving on.

As she waited for her breakfast, she received an email alert on her phone from Sanford Morgan. Or rather, his automated newsletter service. It said he was going to be a guest speaker at an author and reader cruise that was leaving out of Norfolk in a week. It also said there were still a very limited number of cabins still available. Panicked, she raced over to the server and told her to pack her bagel and a coffee to go. She paid, grabbed her order, then hurried out to her car to find her laptop so that she could book one of those remaining cabins.

At the *Cape Charles Coffee House*, Kari Denton looked across the table at Micah, who was wide-eyed. Kari had come up here to check on the investment group's construction project across the street. She had run into Micah who was picking up Sandy's mail. Micah's back was now to the woman who was interrogating the server about Sandy. She started to turn around, but Kari put a hand on her arm to make her stop. Kari held up her phone as if checking a text while stealthily taking a photo of the woman, then she handed it to Micah. She shook her head, not recognizing her. Then their server came over with an apologetic look and motioned that the loud woman must have "issues." By that time, the woman had gone silent.

A few minutes later the woman got up and raced over to the register where she paid and waited for her to-go order. Then she rushed past their table where Micah got a good look at her. Once the woman was out of earshot she said, "I've never seen her before. But these are the kind of things that Sandy has to put up with that drove him down to *Casey's Cove*."

Kari said, "I wouldn't trade places with him on a bet."

"It's why my mom and my aunt had Carol and me, and now just me, stay with him. I was hoping that we were getting past the point of having to worry, but I guess we never will. There are a lot of nuts out there."

Kari nodded. "I'd say that's one of them. At least we have her picture, and so long as she's looking for him up here, she'll never find him. I'll text the picture to Mimi and get her to pass it around to all the *Mallard Cove* wait staff. If anyone spots her, I'll make sure you're notified right away."

In addition to overseeing new developments for the investment group, Kari also oversaw *Mallard Cove* operations. But the group's hotels came under the purview of Cindy Crenshaw, who also ran *Bayside Resort and Club*. Had Kari thought to share it with her to pass down the line to *Mallard Cove Hotel* staff, they would have had a name and address to go with the face. Not that those would have helped much since both were false. But they would've at least known how they'd already dodged a bullet this morning, and that the woman had come within minutes of finding Sandy.

5 THE CLINGER

"I have to tell you, I'm enjoying this. There's something about talking with a woman my own age that's so, well, I want to pick the right word here, and it's somewhere between refreshing and rewarding," Sandy said.

Betsy laughed, "I guess I'll take that as a compliment, especially the part about your being unsure about words."

"Well, you *should* take it as a compliment, because that's how I meant it. I'm the oldest in our little group here, and there's a big difference between the twenty, thirty, and forty-somethings that are part of it and me, being in my late sixties. Hell, the only ones close to my age are Gilligan and his wife Betty, and they're almost ten years younger. Good people, but they still only caught the tail end of the music we both grew up with and the movies we saw back then."

"Gilligan?"

"Captain Bill Cooper. Most everyone calls him 'Baloney' but he likes that, so I call him Gilligan because he hates it."

"I thought you said he and his wife were 'good people.' Why antagonize him?"

Sandy grinned slyly. "Hang around long enough and you'll see. He's got a couple of charter boats in here." He pointed through the window to two empty slips next to the seawall, "But you'll hear him coming long before you even see his boats."

"Why do I feel like you two have some kind of a kind of 'grumpy old men' thing happening?"

"Probably for the same reason that you headed up here after we bumped into each other. Because you're a very perceptive woman." The grin got wider.

Betsy smiled, and there was no blush behind it. "Mimi said you were a 'fishing legend.' I thought you were only known as a fiction writer."

"I started as a guide down in the Keys back when I was a kid, and I was pretty good at it. Made quite a name for myself back then. Some of my clients were very interesting people, and I thought that maybe making up stories about those days would be interesting to other people. That's when I discovered that I was as good or better at a keyboard as I was at poling a skiff, so here I am. Most of the people I deal with now are characters on my computer screen, not flesh and blood. And I've never missed a day of work because of bad weather."

"So why haven't you already gone off into the sunset with a fishing rod in your hand?"

"I could've, especially after that first book was made into a movie. But that's not who I am. I don't write for money anymore; I write because I love it. After my wife died, I leaned on my characters. I could immerse myself in their world, and it was a way of escaping the pain of my own. To me, fiction and books are all about escapism."

"So, I guess now you're ready to leave their world, and that party was part of the plan," she asked.

"No, I'm just going to a different part of their world. And that party was an ambush, I never dreamed my old client would sell me out like that. He said they were 'only going to have a few friends over for a drink or two.' Then you saw how it was a catered cocktail party for over a hundred people, complete with a photographer."

Betsy grimaced. "I wasn't aware of that part, I thought you had known all along. And last week those pictures were in the 'Glossy Sheet,' that society rag."

"I didn't know that, either. Though it doesn't matter, I'm never going back there," Sandy said.

"Funny thing, neither am I. That's part of why I sent the boat ahead, I was busy listing my place down there for sale. I'm tired of all the traffic, and the new people. So many of the crowd that Claude and I were part of are no longer around. The type of life we had doesn't exist there anymore; the island and the lifestyle have changed so much, so fast, and it's depressing. I guess that's why I find this place so appealing, reminding me partly of my past. A fun part, kind of like I'm caught in a time warp. So now I'm carving out a new life and thinking of buying a smaller place somewhere as part of it. Somewhere quieter, more laid back, and north of that madhouse. At least that's the plan today, but like so much else, it's subject to change. Right now, I'm taking life one day at a time. Two weeks ago, I'd never heard of this place, or you. Yet here I am."

He laughed. "And I'd heard of you, I just didn't know it was *you*."

She said, "I take that back. I'd heard of the movies that are based on your books. I just didn't know that you were the one who wrote them."

"I don't know whether to take exception to that or be happy about it. Though you know what? I'm enjoying myself, so I guess it doesn't matter."

"Good, because I am, too. Enjoying myself, that is. And glad that I made this trip."

She wasn't happy about having to use a credit card to book her cabin, though it was a prepaid card, one she could reload. Despite the fact the name on the card was another one she invented, using it still meant leaving a trail of money, both in and out. A trail that could be used to find her again, which was not something she wanted to happen. It was bad enough that she would have to use her brand-new passport with her real name, Donna DuBois when she got to Bermuda. She knew that from that point on she could be tracked.

And speaking of tracking someone, she was frustrated by her lack of leads as to where Sanford's boat could be. His mailing address was here in this town, but his boat sure wasn't. It only made sense that he would use a box in the closest post office to his home, or home port. The problem was, that ESVA was so rural and had such a low population density that there were only a handful of post offices, and each covered a lot of square miles of territory.

She wondered if that picture might not have been taken at some random marina; it might not even have been shot in Virginia. Or maybe he owns some waterfront place around here somewhere. She knew his copyrights were all held by an LLC corporation, meaning there was no way to track him down through them, she'd already tried that. If he had property around here, chances were that it would be held in an LLC, too. Her only lead to his whereabouts was that PO box. She decided to go back in and get a refill on her coffee, then walk the two blocks over to the post office and see what she could find out.

The tables that had been so full just twenty minutes ago were now down to just a couple of older guys conversing loudly about the cobia running down by the tunnel islands, whatever that meant. She got her "to-go" coffee, then headed out for the post office.

A young woman was trying to open the front door while holding one of the big, corrugated plastic tubs with "US Mail" stenciled on all four sides. As she held the door for her, for a split second she thought she saw a spark of recognition on the woman's face. Then she realized she'd seen her earlier in the coffee shop. The woman quickly raised the tub to shoulder height, but not before Donna saw that it was over half-filled with mail.

"Wow. You must've been away for a while."

The woman replied, "A few weeks. That'll teach me to go on vacation I guess." She smiled as she hurried to a car that was parked a few feet away at the curb.

Donna called out, "Need a hand with the car door?"

"Huh? Oh, no, I can manage, but thanks."

Donna went back to her original mission, seeking out Sanford's PO box. Fortunately, this was a very old building, and the boxes were the vintage style with little glass windows in their doors, allowing the renters to look in to tell if they had any mail before they opened them. His was one of the larger boxes, and it was empty. If he was back already, then he had picked up recently and she'd missed him. Or, if he wasn't here yet, maybe they were still holding his mail as they'd been doing for that woman.

For a second, she thought about going to the counter and inquiring about Sanford. But she knew they wouldn't give out any information to an unauthorized person, and she didn't need to add another Federal charge to her list of past transgressions. Instead, she left, thinking while walking back to her car.

Okay, she knew where he was going to be in a week, the same place that she would, be on that cruise ship. The problem was, she didn't know if he was already here in Virginia, or if he was taking his time coming up the coast, going directly to Norfolk.

So, what to do between now and then? Maybe learn as much as she could about the writers he would be meeting up with, the group from *TropicalAuthors.com.* and the other coastal writers. Then she could impress him with her knowledge, maybe help clue him in with names and facts if he didn't know them all. So, she had a week and a half to "cram" like it was a college exam. She'd find a quiet little place with good Wi-Fi to hole up and get started.

Micah went speeding out of Cape Charles, in a hurry to put as much distance between herself and Sandy's stalker as possible. Running into her at the post office was unnerving. Fortunately, she'd had the presence of mind to hold the mail tub high enough so that the woman couldn't read who it was all addressed to and follow her back to *Mallard Cove*. That woman was delusional, claiming that she was a close friend of Sandy's. Micah had never seen her in the two years she had been traveling with him. She was going to show Sandy the picture that Kari had taken, just as soon as she got back to the boat.

Sandy and Betsy walked beyond the boat dry storage barn at the east end of *Mallard Cove*. The fence at the property line had a motorized gate for cars and a pedestrian gate adjacent to it, both equipped with keypad locks. Just beyond the fence were woods, and both the driveway and footpath curved back through those trees, preventing any view of what lay beyond. They walked through the gate and followed the path through the narrow woods line.

As they reached the other side they stopped, letting Betsy take in the view of *Casey's Cove*. In front of them was a long "L" shaped carport that bordered the similarly shaped main floating dock. A variety of boats and house barges were moored side by side there, and Murph and Lindsay's center console, *LNZ II*, was tied up against the seawall on the far side of the basin.

"Cozy little setup you have here. No wonder I couldn't find your boat."

"As I said, the property is Casey and Dawn's, but it's a world all to itself. And you haven't seen the best part yet," Sandy said.

He led her over past the old wooden boathouse and up the concrete walk to *C2*.

"No wonder you were in a hurry to get back here. This place is, well, now it's my turn to be at a loss for words. Gorgeous would be too fluffy, and yet nice isn't fancy enough. Cozy? Comfortable? Inviting? Yes, probably inviting is as close as I'm going to get."

Sandy motioned toward a pair of poolside chairs, and they sat down together. He smiled, pleased that this morning it was like they had picked up their conversation right where they had left off back in Florida.

"Well, hello, who are you," Betsy asked. "He wouldn't be yours, would he?"

KC had walked around from behind her chair. Before Sandy could warn her about not trying to pet him, she was already stroking his head. Then instead of swatting her hand, KC hopped up in her lap.

"That... is KC Shaw. And I don't know if he's mine, or I'm his. I'm stunned though because he never does that."

"Hi... Betsy, isn't it? How did you get KC to do that so fast?" Micah had arrived, surprised to see Betsy with Sandy, and floored to see KC in her lap.

"Hello, Micah. Nice to see you again."

"Likewise... but how did you get to hold..."

Sandy replied, "I was just about to tell her that he normally draws blood when anyone new tries to pet him, much less pick him up, then that happened."

Betsy said, "This sweet guy? I didn't pick him up, hopping up here was all his idea. I like cats though, and this one is very cool." The look on KC's face said, "See? She totally gets me."

Micah shook her head, thinking of how she'd had to work all summer to gain KC's trust. "He's different, even for a cat. And I hate to interrupt you two, but we need to talk about a writing-related security issue, Sandy." She took a seat on the other side of him.

Betsy said, "I'd offer to go and give you two some privacy, but I think this guy has other ideas." KC was now purring loudly.

"Well, it's not like there are any state secrets in this business. What've you got, Micah?"

She pulled the photo up on her phone and then passed it over to Sandy.

"Who's this?" He asked.

"A potential 'phase five clinger.' She was trying to locate you up in Cape Charles, telling anyone who would listen that she's a 'close friend' of yours."

"Never seen her before."

"I thought that was the case."

Betsy chuckled, "Stage five clinger... I loved 'Wedding Crashers.' Great movie."

Sandy said, "It is. And it was filmed a little farther up the Shore in St. Michaels."

"I didn't know that. I may have to take a run up there and take a look around," she said.

"I could be your tour guide. I love that little town."

"That could make it even more fun."

Micah wanted to get back to the subject of the stalker. "Kari sent this picture to all the restaurants and bars here just in case she was to show up. She obviously thought you lived somewhere around Cape Charles, but we can't be too careful."

Betsy asked, "Do you think this woman is dangerous?"

Micah replied, "Most aren't, but it pays to be careful, just in case."

"*Most*? As in, this has happened before?"

Sandy nodded. "It's partly why I moved down here from *Bayside*. People buy a book, then they think that's a license to bug you, twenty-four/seven. Especially up there. Don't get me wrong, I love getting drinks bought for me in bars by my readers. But that doesn't mean it's an invitation to come and sit down at my table and tell me your life story, or worse, follow me back to my boat.

"Up at *Bayside* the DC clientele tends to be more impressed with themselves and think you should be as well. People were climbing onto my boat uninvited to get a book signed and drink some of my beer. It didn't happen as often after I moved down here to *Mallard Cove*, but when Casey offered me a slip over on this side of the fence, I jumped at it. This place is about as private as the waterfront gets around here.

"Most of those people are harmless, just overbearing and irritating as hell. Then there are the occasional ones who are more extreme, delusionally thinking they are part of my life. This woman falls into that group."

Betsy teased him, "I never realized you authors had rock-star-like problems with groupies."

Micah said, "Not all of us, just a select few like Sandy and the other top New York News bestselling authors. He has millions of readers, which means he also has a higher chance of running into an obsessed fan."

Betsy asked, "How about you, Micah? No 'clingers'?"

"Thankfully, no. Though my reader base is only in the tens of thousands so far, and like I said, he has a few extra zeros in his base. Ironically, I work as hard to stay in touch with my readers as he does to hide from his. That's why I'm constantly posting stuff on my social media, just to keep my name out there. I do have a great group of readers who have also become my social media friends. Many of them will be on the upcoming coastal authors' and readers' cruise. This morning Sandy agreed to be our cruise headliner after our main speaker had to cancel."

"I was strong-armed into it. I've never done one before. Normally I hate book signings and personal appearances. And Palm Beach cocktail parties."

Betsy asked, "How were you strong-armed?"

Sandy scowled at Micah, "She asked me to do it. She's my youngest sister's first child, and I never could say 'no' to her, ever since the day she was born. Her mother either, for that matter."

"I wouldn't have asked if we weren't in such a jam, Sandy. I know it's a big ask, and I owe you." Micah looked concerned.

Sandy reached over and gave her a reassuring squeeze of her arm. His voice softened a bit, "You've looked out for me every day for over two years, I guess the least I can do is take this trip with you. But just to make it clear, you're buying your own beer."

She said, "That's a deal."

Betsy asked, "What are the ports of call?"

Micah replied, "We leave out of Norfolk for Bermuda, and then back to Norfolk. All told a four-day cruise. In between grazing at the seafood buffets, we sign books, hold new book readings, and as our headliner, Sandy is going to give the main lecture."

"Wait, I'm going to give a *what*?"

"A lecture. It'll be the main event of the cruise."

"And just what is this lecture supposed to be about," he asked.

"Your latest book, and maybe about the benefits and drawbacks of being a traditionally published versus an independent author? But those are just suggestions, whatever subjects you choose are completely up to you."

"How about one being the dangers of owing favors," Sandy grumped.

"It sounds like fun, Sandy! And Bermuda is great, though I haven't been there in years," Betsy said.

"I've never been there at all. But if it's so great, then why don't you come along? At least that way I'll have someone to talk to about something other than books."

"I would, but the idea of not being able to tell the captain to change our course or the itinerary doesn't work for me. I like cruising on my boat."

Sandy commented, "Yeah, me too. At least it's just under a week."

"So, what's running around here?" Betsy asked.

He looked confused. "You mean, like horse races?"

"No! What kind of *fish* are in right now?"

"Oh, right. Well, Gilligan was crowing about being the cobia king last night, so they must be jumping in the boat these days."

"Good, I love eating cobia. Let's go get some for dinner."

"I would, but I sold my flats boat back in the Keys before we left. I'm going to get a center console, but I haven't had a chance to go look for one yet," Sandy said.

"Well, I brought mine up with me, so we'll use it. Micah, would you like to come too?"

"Thanks, Betsy, but I'll have to take a rain check. I've got a ton of Sandy's mail to get through, and Jeff is coming over this afternoon to give me a hand with washing *Epilogue* after our long trip."

"Do you always jump in and take over like this," Sandy asked, sounding slightly irritated.

"Yes, I do," Betsy replied. "Of course, if you wimp out and don't want to go, you're welcome to stay on the dock."

Sandy quickly replied, "I didn't say that! Yes, I want to go. I'm just used to making my own plans, that's all."

"Well, I am too, so we have that in common. And as nice as it is sitting around here chatting, I've never caught a cobia from a pool chair. Un-ass that seat, and we can continue this conversation on my boat. I'll go break out the tackle and see you on board in ten minutes."

"I'll get some bait and ice from Spud's Trolling Baits. Which means you'll need to bring the beer," Sandy said.

"I wouldn't have expected anything less. See you in ten."

After she left, Micah gave Sandy an amused look. "You have all that beer that Casey gave you yesterday. It's not like you couldn't have taken some of that with you."

He grinned, "This is kind of a test. I want to see what brand of beer she's going to bring. A person's choice of beer says a lot about them."

"You like this lady, don't you?"

"She intrigues me; seems kind of tough, and I like that in a woman. But having spent a grand total of only a few hours with her, the jury's still out. As I said, I want to see what kind of beer she'll bring."

6 BRAND IDENTITY

Sandy was surprised but pleased to find Betsy's cooler loaded with Kalik Gold, an outstanding beer brewed in Nassau, Bahamas. It wasn't even lunchtime yet, and Betsy's rank had already gone up with him by a few notches. At least it had until he tried to take the wheel of the outboard.

"Don't even frigging think about it," she said.

Sandy protested, "You don't know the water around here, but I do."

"Which is why you're the 'nagivator' this morning, so that you can keep me out of trouble."

"You mean navigator."

"No, I said it right the first time. Now how about getting those dock lines."

With a frown, Sandy did as he was asked, then joined Betsy at the lean seat, crossing his arms in protest as she steered them out of the basin.

"Go right after you clear the jetties and aim for the center of Fisherman Inlet Bridge. Then we'll parallel the Chesapeake Bay Bridge Tunnel and run to the tunnel islands. Gilligan said he's been having some luck around there."

She asked, "This Gilligan, he's good?"

"Yes, one of the best, but never let him know I said that."

Betsy chuckled as she advanced the throttles and started her right turn just beyond the jetties. Her center console boat had more power than Murph's *LNZ II* and was over half a dozen feet longer, as well as ten knots faster. The wind had dropped down to a light breeze overnight. There was now only a slight chop in the channel, most of it caused by the outgoing tide pushing against the breeze. Sandy noted that Betsy didn't throttle back to cruise, obviously in a hurry to get to the fishing grounds.

He commented, "This thing moves out, but you know that wide-open-throttle for an extended period like this will take a toll on the life of your engines."

She nodded. "I do know that. But I like fast fishing boats, and I enjoy running them hard. You never know if you might have missed a world record by a minute or two because you slowed down and weren't there when that one big fish came through. It's all about extending the amount of time you keep your lines in the water, and not about extending the life of your engines. They make new engines every day, but world records don't happen often. And I don't want to be late getting to that dance."

Sandy surprised himself by nodding in agreement with her logic. He was discovering there were a lot of things to like about this woman, and not all of them were in her cooler. Even if she wouldn't let him run her boat.

"They seemed to hit it off together down in Florida," Micah said. She and Lindsay were having lunch and catching up at the *Cove Beach Bar*. "For two years I've been helping Sandy fend off the gold diggers and desperate widows. But Betsy doesn't seem to fit into either category."

Lindsay nodded. "And he's the one who chose to go out fishing with her. Quite a sudden change from his old hermit ways."

"He's got KC for company these days, and now that *Epilogue* is moored here permanently, he has the gang to hang out with anytime he wants. Jeff and I have been talking about getting a place together and having me move off the boat. I think Sandy will be okay now without me around all the time. Besides, if he's going to start seeing someone, he'll want more privacy," Micah said.

"They're only going fishing, Micah. I wouldn't count on him getting married off anytime soon."

"I know, I know, but like you pointed out, I've sensed that change in him recently. Not back to being who he was when my aunt was alive, but a definite change. Even more reassured and independent. I'm happy for him and grateful that he's getting his 'mojo' back."

A shadow fell across the table as a large black woman approached them from the beach. Dressed in colorful but earth-toned Caribbean garb, she smiled at Micah. In a soft Haitian accent, she said, "I am Mambo Cecile Jean-Baptiste, but you call me Mama Ceci, as many do, Micah, okay."

Micah was taken aback, "I'm sorry, have we met?"

"No, but we been destined to. Me family owes you Uncle Sandy a life debt from many, many years ago, and de time has come for de repayment, okay." Mama Ceci placed two leather, bead, and shell amulets with leather thong necklaces on the table. "Gris-gris for you and you uncle. Wear dese so no harm come to you both on de watah trip, okay. An' you warn him not to go on dat Stenny boat, an' you neider. Dere be death on dat boat; it be cursed. You tell him all dat, okay. Trust de cat, okay, an' stay off de Stenny boat."

"What's a Stenny boat? Trust the cat? You mean KC?"

"You know soon enough. Wear de gris-gris an you know de bad juju can no harm you, okay. Tell you uncle what I say. Wear de gris-gris, okay." Mama Ceci turned and walked back down the beach, leaving the two bewildered women to stare after her.

Lindsay asked, "Have you ever seen her before?"

"No, never. It seems like ESVA is full of strange women lately. I have no idea who she is, or how she found me."

Lindsay fiddled with her phone and then looked up, surprised.

"Oh, wow, I was looking for that term 'mambo,' but then this popped up." On the screen was a picture of the woman who had just left their table.

"Whoa! So, who is she?" Micah asked.

"According to this, that was Mama Ceci, a well-known mambo from Little Haiti in Miami. A mambo is a voodoo priestess."

Micah's eyebrows shot upward. "A voodoo priestess who knows my name. Here. On ESVA. I thought we left all the weirdness behind, back down in Florida. Life debt? Gris-gris? Trust the cat when I can barely pet him? And what's a Stenny boat?"

Lindsay was back at her phone again. "There's nothing on here about a Stenny boat. Cats and voodoo apparently don't go together, either. And nothing voodoo-centric about a 'life debt,' okay. Just your generic 'I saved your life, now you owe me' kind of thing, okay." She grinned, carrying on with the woman's repetitive use of the word.

"I don't recall Sandy saving anyone's life."

"Maybe not, but she sure did. She's over a thousand miles from home and apparently came here just to warn you and Sandy about a boat. Oh, and to bring you guys these necklaces, okay?" She concentrated on the screen again. "This says that in Haiti, gris-gris are talismans believed to ward off evil spirits. A practice that started in western Africa, centuries ago. I don't know how well they work for that, but they *are* cool looking."

Micah picked up one and studied it. "Lots of work in this, all the little beads are hand sewn."

"Put it on, let's see how it looks."

After tying the leather thong behind her neck, Micah held the amulet between two fingers, striking a pose like a game show model. "Well?"

"Looks good on you! Feel any cosmic vibrations?" Lindsay giggled as she asked.

"Nope, not a thing. So, you must not have bad juju." The two laughed together.

Lindsay said, "I can't wait to see Sandy's face when you give him that. Five bucks say he won't wear it."

"No takers. But he'll get a kick out of it."

⁓

"You're sure her last name is Jean-Baptiste," Sandy asked. He and Betsy had brought their limit of two, four-foot-long cobia to the cleaning table at the end of his dock. KC was perched on one end of the table, semi-patiently waiting for his share.

Micah was surprised, expecting Sandy to have scoffed at the whole story. "Yes... and that's what the Internet said as well. That, and the part about her being a voodoo priestess."

Sandy snorted, "Her voodoo didn't do much for the boy I fished out of the water that day."

"What boy, Sandy?" Lindsay was as much in the dark on this story as Micah and Betsy.

"It was over thirty years ago. I was on the back side of Islamorada, guiding a charter. From up on the poling platform of my skiff, I caught a glimpse of something floating out on the horizon. Back then it wasn't all that uncommon to spot a wayward bale of grass floating out there, and a dry one could've covered my fuel bill for a long time to come. We ran out to it and found this boy, in his early teens. He was unconscious, more dead than alive, but still somehow managing to cling to a small sheet of Styrofoam that had kept him from drowning. He'd been in the water for days, the only survivor of the crowded boat he was on after it sunk at night in a storm. He would never have lived long enough to float from where I found him all the way into shore.

"We pulled the kid onto my skiff, and I hauled ass into the dock, calling for an ambulance on the way. The Coast Guard gave me hell for bringing him ashore, they said I should've radioed them and waited on their boat instead. That way his hitting the beach wouldn't have counted. Back then there was a big hoopla in the courts over interdicting the Haitian refugee boats at sea and sending them back to Haiti. I told that jackass the boy was dying out there on an oversized coffee cup, he wasn't in a damn boat. I said I didn't care where he came from, I'm not leaving anybody out in the water to die, and I hoped somebody would do the same for me if the positions were reversed."

Betsy asked, "So, what happened to him?"

"They stabilized him at Fishermen's Hospital but had to send him up to a hospital in Miami after a strong infection set in. He'd had some nasty, open sores where his skin had been rubbing against the edge of the Styrofoam. A nurse at Fishermen's told me his name was Pierre Jean-Baptiste, and that he had some powerful friends and family in Miami. I never heard anything more about him beyond that. Until now."

"So, this was the 'life debt' she talked about," Micah said.

"Must be. Do me a favor, I've got fish on my hands. You mind tying it on for me?"

Micah started tying the thong as Lindsay asked, "You're going to wear it? You don't believe in voodoo, do you, Sandy?"

"Here's what I believe, I like the looks of that trinket, and I don't want to piss off the voodoo fishing gods if there are such things. So, what the heck, I'll wear it for a while. Adds to the whole 'writer's mystique' look I've got going on."

Betsy laughed and shook her head. "I think it makes you look more like an old hippy surfer."

"I can live with that image, too." He noticed KC staring at the amulet. "What do you think about it, KC? She mentioned you, so you have a say in all this."

The cat walked across the table to get closer to him. He then sat down with his back to the two fish, staring at the leather fob and then up at Sandy.

Micah said, "It has his attention for sure. I've never seen him turn his back on fish before this."

"He'll refocus when we start filleting them, won't you, KC?" Sandy gently pushed him aside and started working on the first fish. The cat did go back to watching his future dinner but stole glances at the amulet in between bites.

∼

According to the social media page, the list of "indie" coastal writers on the cruise was a long one. There was a lot of research to do, but fortunately, they all had decent author pages online. Donna was determined to prepare and become a great resource for Sanford. He was no doubt too busy writing and wouldn't have the time to dig into all this information. Yes, she was going to be invaluable to him, memorizing as much as possible about each author. So far, she'd only managed to research a handful, but soon she would know all there was to know about each of them before the ship left the pier.

First, there was John Cunningham, author of the Buck Reilly series and one of the *TropicalAuthors.com* bunch. A great writer who'd mastered several different careers throughout his life. Started as a bouncer at a disco in Key West back in the 1980s, then eventually became a diver, developer, and pilot. He'd written books, songs, and movie scripts. Talk about an interesting life, it was no wonder he never seemed to run out of inspiration for Buck Reilly because Buck's life was partly based on his.

Then there was Nick Sullivan. In addition to also being a great writer, he was also a multi-talented veteran of stage, screen, television, and audio acting. He created the *TropicalAuthors.com* website. He was an avid SCUBA diver who had logged hundreds of dives throughout the Caribbean and Central America. Many of his books centered around a pair of divemasters, Boone and Emily. She was most surprised to learn that she *knew* him. At least, she felt like she did because she *recognized* him; he had played various parts in several of her favorite television shows. If she hadn't been so dedicated to Sanford, she and Nick would no doubt have become close. But she could only focus on one person, and that was Sanford.

Jinx Schwartz was a TropicalAuthors bestselling writer from Texas who always swore that each new book was going to be her final one. But they never were. Based on the Texas Gulf coast in the winter, she wandered around from state to state in her land-yacht home, named *Po Thang*, in the more temperate parts of the year. But as a ninth-generation Texan, the Lone Star State's coast always called her back home when the snow started falling elsewhere. And she was as sassy as her main character, Hetta Coffey, who appeared in over a dozen books.

Another land-yacht dwelling TA author was Nicholas Harvey, originally from the UK. He and his wife currently lived in the Florida Keys and were avid SCUBA divers, which was undoubtedly why his protagonists were also divers. But while he found excitement these days exploring the undersea world, he used to get his adrenaline fix on ultralight aircraft, hovercrafts, and at over a hundred miles an hour on racetracks. After moving on from motorsports he discovered writing and never looked back.

The more Donna read about the writers in this group the more she realized why they were so successful; their lives were as interesting as those of their characters. However, as great as they all were, Sanford's life and writing beat each of theirs by far. This was why she felt such an attraction and connection to him and was so determined to find him again. If she'd only realized the depth of what they would come to mean to each other when she'd met him at those book signings. It had taken her a while to recognize the magnetic attraction between the two of them, but by then he didn't have any new book signings scheduled.

She realized now it was probably a good thing that she hadn't found him yet. This had given her the time to do her research and memorize all the author bios so she could help him when they met again on the cruise. It's funny how things just seem to come together, she thought. Especially when they're meant to be.

Casey walked down Sandy's dock, spotting him lounging on his aft deck. Sandy waved him aboard and asked, "I don't suppose you brought any beer with you?"

"What happened to the beer I gave you when you got here?"

"I'm conserving it, I don't want to run out. But I guess you can grab us a couple of them while you're up." Sandy motioned to the small aft deck fridge. "I'd get them myself, but he'd object." KC was asleep on his lap.

"Not a problem." Casey withdrew two and handed one to Sandy before taking a chair next to his. "I heard the cobia fishing was good this morning."

"Good enough for dinner and then some."

Casey asked, "Where's your fishing partner?"

"Went back to her boat for a bit. Told her I'd grill up some of the fish in a while over at C2 after we have a swim. She seems to be taken with this place."

"The *Mallard Cove Telegraph* says she seems to be enjoying your company, too."

"Well, then the feeling is mutual. Don't take this wrong, but sometimes it's nice to hang out with someone closer to your own age. That's not a shot at you and Dawn." Casey's wife was over a decade younger than him.

"Didn't take it that way. I get it. There are times when Dawn relates better to Lindsay since they're only a few years apart. But it's not an issue between us."

Sandy took a long sip from his bottle, then looked questioningly at Casey. "What do you know about voodoo?"

"I only know that up until a few hours ago I'd have bet a hundred dollars there wasn't anyone practicing it here on ESVA. But you proved that to be wrong."

"Hey, it wasn't me, I'm not into that stuff!"

"Well, apparently she was here because of you. Micah too, from what I hear. You do have a knack for collecting interesting people, Sandy. Nice necklace you've got there, by the way."

"Thanks, I like it. And I didn't invite her, she just showed up out of thin air. I have no idea how she even knew how to find me; that's strange enough by itself. But everyone around the docks down in Islamorada knew that KC was with me, so her knowing about him isn't that much of a stretch. I guess you heard about the rest of her chat with Micah. I looked up 'Stenny boat' online, and all I found were some naked pagans in a canoe in Germany, and a pier named Stenny in Hamnavoe, which is a UK island in the North Sea, above England. I'm not planning on doing any 'skinny paddling' nor on taking a trip to the UK anytime soon, so I should be safe. But I've got my cat and my new necklace, so I should be good in case I do."

Casey laughed, "You can never take too many precautions around naked pagans with paddles."

"Don't I know it! Bad enough around you and your rag-tag fleet of recycled milk jugs." Sandy wasn't a fan of Casey's band of roto-molded kayak anglers, having turned down numerous invitations to join the group's fishing expeditions, preferring his boats to have both engines and speed. However, he was always open to accepting any of their excess catch, provided that the fish was already cleaned, of course.

"Speaking of which, I'm planning on making a run offshore for some tuna in the morning. Eric Clarke and his daughter Missy are coming along. No naked pagans and we aren't leaving US waters. Care to join us?"

Sandy was excited. "I would, so long as there's no paddling involved. Can I invite a friend?"

"No paddling, we're taking *Predator*. And if you mean Betsy, of course, you can. It would be great for Missy to meet such an accomplished female angler."

Predator was Casey's older fifty-five-foot Jarrett Bay sport fisherman, and Eric Clarke was the 'heaviest hitter' in the investment group that owned *Mallard Cove* and their other waterfront properties. A multi-billionaire who owned the world's largest privately held organic food company, he lived in northern Virginia but had a home at *Bayside Estates*. His daughter Elaina, better known as 'Missy,' was an enthusiastic fifteen-year-old angler who never turned down an invitation to go fishing.

"Great kid, that one. She keeps at it, and she'll be setting records herself pretty soon."

Casey nodded. "I think you're right, and you'd have a tough time trying to stop her. She'd much rather have a fishing rod in her hand than a smartphone."

Sandy snorted, "There's a contradiction in terms, 'smartphone.' Seems like the more these kids use them today, the dumber they get."

"Pretty much," Casey said as he raised his beer in agreement. "I'd rather see kids getting more addicted to fishing than electronics."

7 SETTLING IN

The coastal writers' group's email explained that Travis MacIntosh had fallen ill and wouldn't be able to make the trip. However, as a favor to his niece, Micah Monroe, best-selling author Sandy Morgan would be filling in for him.

This news hit him like a ton of bricks. No wonder that bitch's latest book was trouncing his in the rankings, she must have been riding on her famous uncle's coattails all along. He couldn't recall ever having seen anything linking the two publicly before this, he hadn't even known they were related until now. But it was the only logical explanation for a poser like her to have higher numbers than his. There's no way she should be outselling him, not without help. Without a doubt, her uncle had all the connections she needed.

The email went on to say there would be a dinner with the governor of Bermuda and all the authors. They would be picked up by boat at the cruise ship pier and taken to a waterfront estate for a photo-op for the Bermuda tourism board, then the dinner would follow.

Not exactly what he wanted; having his picture taken with that damn bunch so it could be splashed around the Internet. He wouldn't even be going on this trip except he didn't want them getting even more publicity without him. Though the sales and crooked rankings didn't yet reflect it, his books were so far and above any other writer's in this group except maybe for Morgan's, and he wasn't even sure about his. So now his image would be lost in that crowd, just like his book was. He wasn't a fan of any one of them. By rights, that picture should be just the governor and him.

The email also listed the dress code as cocktail attire for the women, collared shirts, coats, and long pants, or Bermuda shorts for the men. Like he'd ever be caught dead in a pair of those geeky Bermuda shorts. But then a thought hit him, and a plan started formulating in his head. One that would get both him and his book some major headlines, and the sales and ranking it truly deserved. It was ironic; something that he was looking forward to the least might just turn out to be an advantage. A *huge* advantage.

Now he just needed to figure out how to get some special supplies smuggled aboard the cruise ship. That's when he saw the last line of the message. "All books for signings and sale need to be delivered to the ship's loading depot no later than three hours before the ship's departure." Perfect, he thought, problem solved.

The pool temperature was just right; warm enough to be comfortable, but cool enough to be refreshing. Sandy and Betsy were sharing the water with Dawn, who was already in and swimming when they arrived. She asked, "Did you decide to go with them tomorrow, Betsy?"

"Absolutely, I hardly ever pass up a chance to go fishing anymore. I've heard that the tuna fishing off here is second to none in the early spring."

Sandy added, "And I made Casey promise not to bring any of those damned kayaks."

Occasionally they loaded the cockpit of *Predator* with the small plastic boats, launching them along with their anglers when they started seeing fish hitting on the surface offshore.

"He's determined to get you into one," Dawn said.

"Not happening," Sandy said.

She turned to Betsy, "What about you, Betsy? Ever do any kayak fishing?"

"Not yet, though the whole 'mother ship' idea Sandy talked about sounds intriguing to me, even if it doesn't to him. Getting down on the same level as the fish would make it a lot more challenging. But I'm looking forward to fishing on your Jarrett Bay tomorrow. I've never been aboard one, though I've seen a couple at tournaments. Beautiful lines, and that great Carolina flare on her bow."

"Thanks. She's not as fast as most of the newer ones, but at least she's a proven fish raiser."

"Are you going too?"

"Not this time, Eric's girlfriend Candi and I already had plans to go over to Virginia Beach for some shopping and lunch. But we'll get out there together on another day. By the way, we're building quite a women's fishing team here at *Mallard Cove*, and I think you'd like everyone on it if you want to join in. We'll be entering some of the mid-Atlantic tournaments this summer if you're planning on still being here."

"I'll probably be here, and that sounds like it could be fun."

The sound of an approaching helicopter distracted them. They watched as Eric's red and white Sikorsky S-76 came in and landed on *C2's* helipad between the pool and the edge of the Virginia Inside Passage. Two of Dawn and Casey's crew members were standing by to carry Eric, Missy, and Candi's bags over to *Lady Dawn*, where the arriving trio would be spending the night.

As they approached the pool Sandy scowled at Eric, "Do you have to make so damn much noise every time you come here, Clarke? Why can't you come in on something quieter; like say, a straight-piped Harley."

Eric glared right back at him. "I do it specifically to annoy you, Morgan. And by the way, welcome back to ESVA, you old coot."

"I only came back because I heard you were bringing in a load of beer with you on that eggbeater."

"You wish, suds scrounge."

Betsy was standing in the shallows, mouth slightly agape. She had heard of Eric Clarke down in Palm Beach, where he had a winter home. But this Eric Clarke didn't resemble the description of the one in Florida, who was known around the island to be mostly quiet and very crowd shy. Down there, the only parties he attended were smaller, more intimate ones that had some connection to his business. Other than that, he remained mostly a recluse.

Seeing her reaction, both men broke into large grins. Sandy said, "Eric, Candi, Missy, this is Betsy."

"Pay no attention to these two, Betsy. They're just playing. It's what they do," Candi said.

"Hi, Sandy!"

"Hello, Missy, I'm happy to hear that we'll be fishing together again."

"I know, it's great! I'm glad you're back, and I hope we'll get a chance to fish a lot more this season."

"Count on it, kiddo. That's what summers are for."

"I just finished your latest book, and I loved it. I especially liked the character of the young girl who solved the mystery, since she fishes a lot."

"Well, you should've liked her; she's based on you."

"Really? She is? That is so cool!"

"You should always write about what you know if you want your readers to feel a connection to the story. So far, judging by the reviews, they're connecting well with 'your' character. And by the way, that might not be the last book where she appears." He winked at her.

"That's awesome!"

Betsy smiled at Sandy, not having heard about this before, and surprised that he had connected so well with a teenager. She was now looking forward to seeing the two of them fish together.

"Well girls, let's go get changed into some swimsuits. That water looks too inviting to pass up," Eric said.

"Casey's on the boat putting on his suit as well, and he'll be here shortly," Dawn said.

"In that case, we'll hurry back before all the good pool chairs are gone," Eric joked.

After they disappeared down the path, Betsy said, "Eric Clarke isn't at all like I expected."

Dawn said, "That's because this is one of the few places where he can be himself and relax. Plus, he loves watching Missy fish more than anything else, and he's proud of her. Deservedly so, too. Over the past two years, she's become quite the accomplished angler. She has her own outboard up at *Bayside*, and she goes out with us on *Predator* quite a bit. Enough that Eric has been talking about getting a sportfishing boat of his own."

"Betsy, wait until you see her on white marlin using light tackle. Very impressive kid, and that's why it was so easy to create a character based on her. She's got a heck of a future ahead; she's as sharp as her old man, and has the fishing instinct of a tournament winner," Sandy said.

"Don't forget, she got her first white marlin in a kayak, Sandy." Dawn loved needling him on this point.

That raised Betsy's eyebrows. "Really? A white from a kayak? How? Did you drag the kayak behind the mother ship while she trolled a bait and then cut her loose to fight it?"

"No. We were offshore, fishing for mahis. We found a wide and long weed line, so we launched the kayaks to paddle along it. We dropped in some live bait and were surprised when we had a couple of whites come up on them. You should have seen the look on her face, and Eric's."

"I bet, Dawn. Yes, I'd love to try offshore fishing from a kayak this summer. That's something completely new to me."

Sandy winced, looking like he'd bitten into a lemon.

Dawn smirked, "Hear that, Sandy? Betsy is interested in expanding her fishing horizons, so why aren't you?"

"Because I don't have a damn death wish, that's why."

Betsy tilted her head slightly, challenging Sandy. "Where's your sense of adventure?"

"I left it on the nightstand next to my bunk, attached to my survival instinct."

"Funny guy. Seriously? You wouldn't go with me to do some kayak fishing? I didn't chase you all the way up here just to have you wimp out on me."

"Chase me up here?"

"Remember what I said this morning about time being more valuable at our age, and missing out if you just sit around? Don't overthink things, Sandy, be a bit more impetuous and adventurous. Take a risk now and then. I did by coming up here. Now I'm hoping it wasn't a thousand-mile mistake." She cocked her head slightly, waiting for some kind of answer.

Dawn had retreated to the pool steps, not wanting to be in the middle of an argument, but not wanting to miss one if it happened, either. Besides, it was her pool, and she wasn't about to go anywhere.

"I told you this morning that I liked your company. However, that doesn't mean I'm going to let you shove me into a recycled milk jug to go bobbing around, sixty miles offshore. But I'll watch you while you do it. Somebody has to man the cockpit and hand out the equipment. That, and call the Coast Guard to get help locating the bodies..."

"Dawn, sign me up for the next time you go out with the kayaks," Betsy said, not showing any signs of backing down.

While she normally wouldn't want to get into someone else's argument, Dawn was tired of Sandy continually taking shots at kayak fishing without ever having tried it. "Done. Have you ever been out on a kayak before?"

Betsy nodded. "I have, but I've never fished from one. That must be hard, having to paddle to move while dealing with a fishing rod too."

Dawn nodded, "That's part of what makes it fun and challenging. Lots of variables. We'll watch the weather and the fishing reports for the next few weeks and pick our day."

Betsy gave Sandy her most triumphant look before submerging and swimming the length of the pool underwater.

Donna continued her research into the other authors that were going on the trip.

Armand Rosamilia. Now there was a very interesting writer, she thought. A Florida transplant from New Jersey, he was one of the *TropicalAuthors.com* group. With his bald head and uber-long goatee/beard, he looked more like a frontman for a heavy metal band than a guy whose backlist of books took up thirteen pages on Amazon (if you included all his anthologies.) Though when he donned one of his favorite do-rags, he looked like he would make a perfect pirate figure for the Blackbeard Festival at the Hampton waterfront.

From his social media, she quickly determined he had a penchant for great diner food and rare liquor. He seemed like a character that Sanford would invent, so she made a mental note to make sure the two got introduced.

Jack Hardin. A multi-series writer from the west coast of Florida via Texas, he came out of nowhere and quickly became a full-time and very popular and successful independent writer. He was also part of that TA website group. He was into the martial arts, something she would be certain to point out to Sanford, in case he ever needed a good reference source for research.

Kirk Jockell. A retired US Navy Senior Chief from the Florida panhandle, his Navy years provided an intimate knowledge of the water around Norfolk and Virginia Beach. He looked like a cross between a younger Sam Elliott and Tom Selleck from back in his Magnum PI years. Jockell had quickly produced over a half dozen novels and novellas, and neither his sales nor writing had shown any signs of slowing down, except when a new coastal brewery opened. He was recently added to the TA website. He would be a great local

Chesapeake knowledge source for Sanford and became another one added to her list of favorites.

Chris Niles. Quite an interesting woman. Her picture on the TA website looked like she could be Julia Roberts's younger sister. Judging from the rankings of her half-dozen books, she was somewhere in the top five percent or so of Amazon's authors. She was obsessed with the southwest Florida coast, and SCUBA diving. Her writing style was easy and free-flowing, and her characters spoke as real people do. Very interesting, she killed off her protagonist's husband in a home invasion, allowing her to... *move aboard and "live the free and easy" boat life.* Oh, hell no! There was no way she was going to let this woman get within a hundred yards of Sanford! His lifestyle couldn't be more tailor-made for what was obviously her idea of nirvana, and he would be an easy target for a conniving woman like her. No way in hell she was letting that happen.

As so often occurred at *C2*, one person's idea to cook out became the inspiration for others at *Casey's Cove* to join in. Sandy and Betsy's cobia was soon joined by a variety of "bring what you have" meats and seafood for the grill, along with vegetable sides and salads for sharing. Betsy had been surprised and impressed with the atmosphere that seemed to be like a dock party crossed with a family reunion. While *Mallard Cove* had quickly grown on her, she'd completely fallen in love with *C2*. It was such a great bonus to those people living on the docks here, and a real plus for the friends of the Shaws who got to share it with them.

The folks in *Casey's Cove* were all so warm and outgoing. In addition to Clarke's group and the Shaws at the dinner tonight, there had been Marlin and Kari Denton, along with Lindsay and Murph. She found all their backstories interesting, and so fitting with the rest of the atmosphere. Even if Betsy hadn't been attracted to Sandy at the party in Palm Beach and followed him up here, and had instead met all of them separately, she felt certain that they would've become her friends anyway.

She sat on the aft deck of *Cheri*, having a nightcap by herself. Sandy had walked her back to the boat but declined an invitation to join her for one last drink. Maybe he was gun-shy, she thought and had misconstrued the full intent of the invitation. Which had been that drink, and only that drink. Perhaps down the way, there might be more to a similar invitation, but for now, that was the extent of it. Besides, they were set to leave the dock at dawn, and she needed a full night's sleep. By herself.

8 BOATS TO BUILD

Betsy climbed aboard *Predator* just a bit before daylight. The generator and the MAN diesel engines were already running, warming up for the long offshore run. Climbing the steps and going into the cabin she found Jeff, the captain. He motioned to a pile of recently made sticky buns on the galley counter, and a pair of stainless-steel commercial pump airpots alongside them, filled with piping hot coffee. He told her to help herself.

"So, you bake as well as find fish," Betsy joked.

He laughed, "No, ma'am. The *Cove Restaurant* just delivered everything, including our lunch."

"Ma'am is just wrong; please call me Betsy." She took a bite of one of the warm buns and rolled her eyes. "Even if we don't catch anything, it was worth getting up early for one of these."

"Yes, ma... er... Betsy. They only make them on the weekends; they're great hangover cures, or so they claim," he grinned. "But Casey considers them good luck."

"Because they *are* good luck!" Casey came through the cabin door along with Eric, making a beeline for the sweet pastries. "Good morning you two, and you'll see what I mean when we get out there, Betsy."

Eric chimed in, "What he means is that the tuna run is so hot right now it's hard to get skunked. Which makes a great excuse for adding in these extra carbs and calories."

"Where's Missy? I'm looking forward to chatting with her." Betsy told Eric.

He replied, "In the cockpit, talking with Micah and Sandy, catching up on this past winter's happenings."

"I'm about to put them both to work, handling the dock lines," Jeff said. "Since everyone's aboard, we'll get going. We have a long run ahead."

The sun was just breaking over the horizon as land disappeared behind them. Everyone was up on the flying bridge for the two-hour ride out to the fishing grounds. Though *Predator* was capable of a thirty-knot cruise, Jeff had her backed down to just under twenty-five knots. They were headed almost straight into six- to eight-foot swells, which were bunched close together, not the most comfortable of conditions. But the boat's famous Carolina flare bow was keeping them dry as it rode over one wave after another.

"If we were on Murph's Merritt, we'd be taking spray up here on the bridge right now," Casey said. "When I was a kid back in Florida, I never understood the big bow overhangs of the Carolina boats. I thought they were so ungainly compared to the more knife-style bows of the Ryboviches, Andy Mortenson's, and Merritts. It's funny how the waves can be so different from one place to another, and how this influences boat design and construction."

Eric nodded. "Jarrett Bay has adapted well to these waters."

Casey looked back at their wake and noticed a boat on a parallel course that must've come out of Rudee Inlet or Lynnhaven. It appeared to be overtaking them. "We've got company, Jeff."

Jeff looked back and stared at the oncoming boat with a dark blue hull. "Looks like *Steel Leader*, a seventy-foot Jarrett Bay that's owned by one of the marine engine manufacturers. I heard she was over at Lynnhaven. I wanted to go have a look at her, but I haven't had time yet."

"What's kept you so busy," Casey asked. He winked at Micah who was in the navigator seat next to Jeff.

Jeff ignored the jab by his boss and said, "She's got that new Furuno Omni sonar system installed."

Casey nodded and said, "Nice."

Eric asked, "What's so special about this Furuno thing?"

Casey replied, "It's basically an inverted periscope for sonar. When they slow to trolling speed, they extend an eight-inch periscope down through the hull a few feet and it lets them see a swath up to a quarter-mile wide, from the surface down to the bottom."

"What's so different about that from the sonar you already have?"

"Our fish finder sonar scans in an inverted 'V' pattern. Meaning we can see a lot of fish down toward the bottom, but up by the surface they need to be directly underneath us or we'll miss them. You could have a trophy fish swimming parallel to you and you'd never know it. This changes all that and even gives you the ability to lock onto a large fish or school and track them. Then you can get out in front of the fish with your baits instead of just blind-trolling," Casey replied.

"All the top tournament boats are getting these, and most of the serious new boats are being built with them. Their screens update every half second," Jeff said.

Casey added, "I looked into adding it, but it would cost around a hundred fifty grand to retrofit this boat with one. And since she's already two decades old, it's not worth it. That's part of why I was thinking about getting a new boat."

Eric glanced over and was surprised to see that *Steel Leader* had caught up to them and was passing abeam. Her captain waved as she shot on by at nearly twice their speed, barely pounding in the big swells.

Jeff said, "That is one beautiful rig. Twenty percent larger fishing cockpit, the Furuno sonar, Seakeeper gyro stabilizer, and one and a half times our normal cruising speed. He didn't even need to back down at all in these swells." The envy in his voice was obvious.

"What is she, twenty feet longer than us?" Eric asked.

"Fifteen," Casey answered. "But the biggest difference isn't the length of her hull, it's the design and build. Much lighter than us, with tunnels for the running gear and flatter shaft angles." When Eric looked confused, he said, "Makes her faster and more fuel efficient."

"You know the boat that well?"

"I looked into getting a new one built. Then I found out they have a very similar seventy-footer down at their boatyard in North Carolina that's a stalled project. The customer is in the middle of an unexpected divorce and needs cash. The engines are already in, as are dual generators, a Seakeeper gyro, that Furuno sonar, refrigerated in-deck fish boxes, the works. And the Furunos now have a six-month waiting list for delivery. They had just gotten set the wheelhouse on this boat when the guy told them he had to stop. It's a steal at what he's asking, but I couldn't justify the cost," Casey said.

Eric looked thoughtful, realizing the full depth of knowledge and expertise shared between Casey and Jeff. He looked at Casey and asked, "What about justifying half?"

That caught Casey off guard. "Go in on it together?"

"Yes. Missy does most of the fishing in our family, and she usually goes offshore with you guys. You're talking about doing tournaments and including her, so why not?"

"Because I've never shared ownership of a boat with anyone before. I've always been the sole owner of my boats and made all the decisions about their maintenance, what tournaments I wanted to fish, and the works. I don't know how well I'd like sharing one, even if it's with you."

"What if you were to still handle all the maintenance, and we work out a tournament schedule together? Missy is the only tournament angler in our family, and we always fish with you on your boat anyway. This would just be a way for me to share the cost and feel less like a freeloader. Just think about it," Eric encouraged him. "If it doesn't work out, I'll agree to buy you out of it at what you've got in it."

"Okay, I'll think about it, and talk it over with Dawn. But you guys are never 'freeloaders.' We like having you along anytime you want to go."

"Thanks. But this would make me feel more comfortable doing that. Just consider it, that's all I ask."

Sandy and Betsy were sitting together across from Eric and Casey, and like everyone else on the flybridge, they couldn't help but overhear their conversation. Sandy said, "I've seen a few boat partnerships that worked well, but mostly I've seen them go south, and fast. I'd hate to see that happen to you two."

Eric said, "We're already partners in several properties and businesses. Casey knows from those that I leave the management to him, but he also knows he can depend on me to write my share of the checks when needed. The same thing would go for any boat we'd own together. He knows a lot more about the sportfishing world than I do, and I'd be getting all that expertise as part of the deal. And I bet most of the partnerships you've seen go sour did so because of money, or an inadequate partnership agreement. Neither of those reasons would be an issue here."

Sandy didn't look convinced, but Eric saw Missy was extremely excited at the prospect of having part of a large sport fisherman. It was the ultimate tool in any serious fisherman's arsenal. Truthfully, he would probably go ahead and buy the boat himself if Casey and Dawn declined, but he liked spending time with them and being involved in business together.

As with all their properties and deals, Casey would bring a lot to the table if they did this together, and Jeff was a great captain. They would no doubt keep any new boat in *Predator's* slip, and this would give Eric a place to stay inside *Casey's Cove* that he would own part of. As it was now, he had to borrow accommodations on *Lady Dawn*, or drive back and forth to *Bayside* on fishing days. Flying in before dawn in his helicopter wouldn't make him any friends with the folks there who were still sleeping.

He saw Casey was texting back and forth with someone, and he looked up a minute later.

"Dawn is open to the idea. I'm not a hundred percent convinced, but I'm leaning toward it."

Eric beamed, "Great! You want to run down and look at it tomorrow?"

"They aren't normally open on Sunday, but I can text and see if they'll accommodate us."

"We can take my helicopter."

Now it was Casey's turn to smile since he loved riding in the Sikorsky. "I was hoping you'd say that."

Donna had dug into more of the writers, working her way down the list. With so many of them booked on the cruise, they had attracted well over a couple of hundred people, making this seem more like a floating mini-convention of coastal book readers. She knew she was going to have her hands full, making sure that no pushy people got near Sanford. She was dedicated to protecting the man at all costs.

The backgrounds of this group of coastal writers were about as diverse as they came. Douglas Pratt was a *TropicalAuthors.com* writer and sailor who wrote short stories and poems before hitting a home run with his Chase Gordon Tropical Thrillers. Ironically, he lived on a farm in Tennessee with horses, goats, cats, and dogs. When not on his sailboat he was about as far removed from coastal life as it got.

Stewart Matthews was another poet from back in his high school days. He became a freelance journalist before teaming up as a co-author with one of the highest-ranked coastal writers and joining TA. In addition to numerous other books, he wrote the popular Cready Marsen series.

What was it with coastal writers being poets or Tennesseans, she wondered? David Berens, another TA member, settled in Knoxville after having spent time up and down the southeast coast of the US. He'd had a long career teaching tennis and now wrote the highly successful Ryan Bodean TropiThrillers.

Evan Graver was a very interesting TA character. Paralyzed in a motorcycle accident while in the Navy, he then bounced from career to career until he started writing. The wheelchair never held him back, however. From jumping out of perfectly good airplanes to diving deep under the ocean's surface, he managed to squeeze every drop of gusto out of life. After becoming a SCUBA diving fanatic, he moved to Hollywood, Florida. He now dived at least once a week when he wasn't writing the Dark Series, which featured his Ryan Weller character. She decided he was someone whom Sanford should also get to know.

Then there was Chip Bell, a successful personal injury lawyer from Pennsylvania. When not busy in court, he wrote the Jake Sullivan series, over a dozen of them so far. A TA writer, he'd also developed one movie script and a TV pilot script based on his book series. He had lots in common with Sanford.

Presley Peterson. She wondered why he was even on this cruise. With only one self-published book to his name which was now over five years old and having accumulated only a handful of mostly low ratings, he didn't appear to be a serious writer. His author page and website had been touting the "imminent release" of "the highly anticipated sequel" for over two years. Meaning that it probably didn't exist. Most of the pictures on his web pages were taken by professional photographers. It was a collection of Presley posing in front of boats, airplanes, and exotic cars set in expensive-looking locations. Real ego-centric photos; more like what you'd see in an actor's portfolio than a writer's. Maybe if he spent more time learning to write and less time preening, he might sell a few books, she thought.

Micah Monroe. A pretty young woman and an interesting writer with a promising series and career. Coincidentally, she saw that Micah also lived on the Eastern Shore of Virginia, just like Sanford did in the summer. She wondered if the two might ever have bumped into each other. She'd be sure to ask Sanford, and if not, she'd make sure they were introduced. Then she realized there was something familiar about her... she was that woman at the post office in Cape

Charles! It was her; she was certain of it. If she'd only known who she was then, they could've had a wonderful conversation about her life as a writer on the Eastern Shore. This would've helped Donna even more to prepare before meeting up with Sanford.

The seas hadn't lain down at all. Despite the fact they had a seventeen-foot beam, this wasn't a match for the swells when they were in the trough. *Predator* was getting tossed around as waves repeatedly hit them broadside. Everyone had to hang onto whatever they could grab when moving about, as the boat rolled back and forth. The best place to be right now was sitting down, or at least within easy reach of something stable.

Missy was camped out in the fighting chair with Micah hanging onto the chair back to steady herself. Sandy, Betsy, Casey, and Eric were all wedged into the bench seat on the mezzanine deck, up against the cabin bulkhead, a couple of feet above the fishing cockpit's deck.

While the rough water was a nuisance, the tuna were biting, and it was well worth putting up with the discomfort. They already had several "keeper" bigeye tuna in the fish box, and it was only ten a.m. *Steel Leader* was aft of them and slightly to the side, headed in their direction.

Jeff called down from the flybridge, "He's cutting it as close to us as he can; he must see something on his Furuno."

Just then the right flatline started screaming, and Missy transferred the rod from the fighting chair's side holders into its center gimbal. The fish was taking a lot of line, and fast. While he'd have liked to have kept trolling the additional lines, Jeff quickly figured this was a big fish. Unless they stopped to fight this one, all of Missy's fifty-pound test line could be gone shortly.

"Clear the rods, we're going to have to be able to turn to get on this one," he shouted as the bench emptied. Everyone was grabbing rods and reeling furiously.

Sandy was reaching over to put a rod in a holder at the front of one of the covering boards when the boat took an unexpected lurch. Both he and the rod went flying, and he ended up down on the deck, the back of his head impacting the teak sole with a sickening "thud."

Betsy rushed over, expecting him to be unconscious or at least stunned, but he looked up and said, "I'm fine. Just take this damn thing so I can get back up," and he handed her the rod.

Casey had started across the cockpit, relieved that his friend didn't appear to be seriously hurt and that only his ego seemed to be wounded. Looking past Sandy, he saw that *Steel Leader* now had what appeared to be multiple hookups. Her captain had also stopped to give his crew time to stow the extra rods. But unlike *Predator*, she was barely rocking, just riding up and down on the swells like an elevator while staying level.

Eric had noticed, too. "That's one stable boat."

Casey nodded. "It's that Seakeeper gyro. Kills most of the roll when you're in the trough."

Now that the other lines were out of the way, Jeff turned and backed down slightly on their fish. Fortunately, it had taken a direction that led them away from the other boat and it had now started to sound. Missy was concentrating on getting her line back, and she was beginning to make progress. It was obvious that this was a very big tuna. One of the fastest and strongest species of fish in the Atlantic, tuna are streamlined speedsters that can wear out the most seasoned angler. They can reach speeds of almost fifty miles per hour, even faster than *Predator* at wide-open-throttle, and yet they can cross entire oceans. The fight itself is worth the cost and effort put into chasing them, but of course, fresh tuna is considered to be the "Kobe beef of the sea."

Missy fought the fish for almost a half hour before Micah announced, "Color!" Meaning, she could see the shiny skin of the fish against the deep blue water of Norfolk Canyon. She now donned a pair of canvas work gloves to keep her fingers from being cut by the leader when she grabbed it and wrapped it around her hands.

"Casey, get that long gaff," she asked, after seeing that it was a huge yellowfin tuna. It was going to take the two of them working together to get this one into the boat.

"Over the side, or through the door?" he asked.

"This one looks like a gut strainer, let's not take any chances. We'll pull it through the door instead of over the gunwale," she replied.

"I'll get the door open after I get a gaff in it."

The door they were talking about was in the stern of the boat, right above the waterline. About three and a half feet across and two feet high, it had originally been designed for ease of hauling in large tuna and billfish. Tuna doors, or as they are also known, transom doors, had replaced cockpit block and tackle gin poles from the old days that were so cumbersome and slow. It was a lot easier to pull a fish through the door at the surface level than it was to hoist it a dozen feet into the air on a rocking boat to get it over the gunwale. And on a rough day like today, hoisting anything this heavy would be dangerous.

Micah now had the thick monofilament leader wrapped around one glove as she moved in to get another handful, farther down by the fish. As she pulled it closer to the transom, Casey stroked the tuna with his long gaff. The fish went into a frenzy, trying to make one last mad dash to escape, almost pulling Casey along with it. Eric came up beside Micah and stroked the fish with another gaff. With the second gaff through its body, the tuna was now resigned to its fate, all its fight having been spent. Casey passed his gaff to Micah then carefully made his way over to the transom door.

He unhooked the latch under the covering board, then reached over the stern to take control of the door. Unfortunately, at that moment *Predator* fell off the side of a large wave, knocking Casey off his balance and making the heavy wood door swing wildly, catching his hand between it and the transom.

"Arghhhhh," he cried out as his hand was crushed. He pulled it out from between the two, managing to secure the door open with his other hand and hooking the restraining strap.

"You all right?" Eric looked concerned.

"Yeah, fortunately, I was born with a spare," Casey replied ruefully, holding up his uninjured hand.

Micah and Eric maneuvered the big tuna over to the door. Casey used his good hand to reach through the open door and attach a stainless meat hook into the tuna's lower jaw, then he and Micah pulled it through the door together. Jeff looked down from the bridge rail and let out a whoop. "Nice yellowtail, Missy, that'll top a hundred pounds, easy!"

Missy glowed from the praise. This was her largest tuna to date and an easy Virginia citation catch. Sandy was standing behind her fighting chair and added, "We've got to get you on some giant bluefin tuna; you're ready."

"Thanks for getting it aboard everybody, that was a fun fight. Sandy, are you okay? It sounded horrible when your head hit the deck." As happy as she was with the fish, she was worried about her friend.

"Didn't even hurt," he assured her. But as they resumed trolling and everyone worked to get the baits back out, Casey insisted on checking him over. They sat on the mezzanine bench where Casey looked for any signs of a concussion. But Sandy's irises looked the same, his memory was sharp, and most amazingly, he didn't even have a bump or a bruise.

Casey said, "That's incredible. Honestly, when you hit the deck, it sounded like someone hitting a home run. How you don't have a knot on your head, a splitting headache, and scrambled brains is beyond me."

Sandy rubbed his fingers over his new shell amulet. "I guess I'm protected," he grinned.

"Yeah, right. If that thing kept you from getting hurt, you would've figured it should've prevented your fall in the first place."

"Ah! Don't doubt the power of my new gris-gris," he chuckled.

Casey shook his head. "Well, Micah's worked better; she's still on her feet."

"Yes, and she's four decades younger than me, too. Not better gris-gris, just better, more youthful, balance. And how's your hand?"

Casey held it up, two of the knuckles had a bluish cast to them. "It hurts, but nothing is broken. I guess I could've used some gris-gris of my own," he joked.

Later in the day, they headed back to shore, wanting to reach the scale at the marina while it was still light. They had plenty of tuna to share among all the folks in *Casey's Cove*, as well as with Betsy and her crew. While everyone else was up top on the flybridge, Casey and Eric were on the mezzanine bench, talking.

"Sandy's fall scared the heck out of me," Casey said.

"Rough day," Eric replied.

"Yeah, but..."

"I know what you're going to say. He might not have fallen if we'd been on *Steel Leader*."

Casey nodded. "Lots of difference between these two boats, and not just the fifteen feet of length."

"Twenty years of difference in technology. I was thinking about that too. A rough day like today can wear you out, but I guarantee those guys aren't nearly as tired as we are. It was amazing watching how stable she is," Eric said.

"As the years go by, everybody loses a bit of balance, and at some point, it'll be our turn, Eric. The more stable a platform we have, the fewer days we'll need to stay at the dock because it's too rough. More and more boats are getting equipped with gyros; the new boat market is demanding it, even in smaller center console outboards. And while I might be able to squeeze a gyro into this boat, it's better when the hull is originally designed and built around it, so that the stresses are spread out more evenly. And again, it's money that I wouldn't get back by putting one in here because of this boat's age."

Eric nodded, "All the more reason to make that trip tomorrow morning."

Up on the flybridge Jeff said, "I can't believe you weren't knocked out cold. I heard your head hit, all the way up here."

"Just hardheaded, I guess, but I swear, it doesn't even hurt. I guess it sounded a lot worse than it was," Sandy shrugged.

"Then it looked that way, too. I've seen people get knocked out when they took a fall on a teak deck; it's not a very forgiving wood," Betsy said.

"That's because I'm tougher than anybody else you know."

"Hardly. But I must admit, I didn't think anyone would get right back up after a fall like that. So, maybe you are, after all."

9 IT TAKES TUNA TO TANGO

Missy's yellowfin weighed in on the *Mallard Cove Marina* scale at a hundred and seven pounds, far short of the state record, but large enough for a Virginia citation. A picture was taken of the huge fish hanging on the scale with all of them standing beside it, to be added to *Mallard Cove's* website as well as the *ESVA Telegraph*. Then they reloaded the fish onto *Predator* for the short trip around to *Casey's Cove*.

All the tuna were laid out beside the fish cleaning station next to the boathouse. Casey turned on the overhead lights to counter the growing dusk. Under the watchful eyes of KC, Jeff and Casey worked on all the bigeye tuna first, filleting and bagging the beautiful bright red loins from each. Well, almost all the loins made it into the bags; some were minus small portions they nicknamed the "cat tax." Then Sandy and Eric walked up the dock, each carrying an extra beer for the two of them.

Casey said, "Let me guess, these are from *Predator*, not *Epilogue*."

Sandy replied, "Of course they are! I have to be careful with mine, I'm running low."

"Are you already into that second case I gave you?"

"Well... no. But I'm in 'conservation' mode. You can't be too careful with Baloney around you know, he's the biggest beer mooch." Sandy replied.

"I've heard he has competition," Casey said sarcastically. When Sandy ignored him, he and Jeff went back to their work of filleting the rest of the bigeye. Then came time to lift the big yellowfin onto the cleaning table. Casey took the head while Jeff and Eric had the tail.

"Careful with it, you don't want to lose it over the side," Sandy warned.

Eric said, "You could help, you know."

"Well, I could, but after that knock on the head, I might be prone to getting woozy. I wouldn't want to be the reason it went overboard. Hey, be careful, lift your end higher, Casey!"

Missy rushed down the dock to help Casey lift the tuna's head. It wasn't that it was so heavy as it was awkward and slippery. "Sorry to be late, I was helping wash the boat."

Casey said, "That's okay, Missy, you were doing something else to help out." He scowled at Sandy.

Sandy said, "Hey! I brought you a beer, didn't I?"

"Yeah, one of my own!"

"Sheesh, I didn't realize you were so territorial about these things. You're starting to sound like Gilligan."

Casey shook his head and started slicing into the huge fish. The meat in this yellowfin was beautiful, much lighter in color than the bigeyes, more toward pink than bright red. They would save the forward belly meat for sashimi later this evening after it had a chance to cool down on a bed of ice. No part of today's fish would go to waste; even the leftover filleted carcasses would go over to *Spud's Trolling Baits* to be ground up and sold as chum.

They all split up the tuna and headed back to their boats. Both the rough day and the sunshine had taken their toll on everyone. Most of them had a morning flight down to Beaufort, North Carolina, and would turn in early tonight.

The next morning Sandy was having breakfast out on the *Cove's* outside deck when Betsy came walking down the charter dock. He waved her over.

"Hey, good morning," she said as she approached.

"To you as well."

"How's your head, did you sleep all right?"

He nodded, "Like the dead. I think I've found the cure for insomnia; a voodoo charm and a rap on the head."

"It might've had more to do with that rough day yesterday."

"Probably. But what a great day of tuna fishing. We even made the paper." He showed her the tuna and crew pictured in the *ESVA Telegraph*.

Their server appeared and started to hand Betsy a menu, but she waved it away and asked, "Do you have sticky buns this morning?"

"They just came out of the oven."

"I'll have one and a cup of coffee."

After the server left, Betsy refocused on Sandy. "Speaking of tuna, would you care to help me grill some onboard *Cheri* this evening?"

"I can do that."

Their conversation was interrupted again, this time by the distant sound of a helicopter. They watched as Eric's Sikorsky appeared above the high tree line that hid *Casey's Cove* from the marina. It gained altitude and speed as it headed south out over the water. They watched as it paralleled the mouth of the Chesapeake and was soon out of sight.

She said, "I'm surprised you aren't with them."

"I'm sure it won't be the last time they'll be running down there, and I'll have another opportunity. They didn't need me to get in the way today, and besides, I already had plans for the day."

"I'm sure they wouldn't think of you as being 'in the way.' But I'm disappointed that you're busy. Since you didn't go with them, I thought I might ask you if you'd like to spend the day with me."

He smiled, "That was what I already had planned to do. I thought I'd show you around the Shore a bit."

"Perfect! That's exactly what I had in mind. Wait, 'another opportunity?' So, you were invited to go with them today?"

"Eric asked me last night, but I told him I was busy."

"What if I had been busy?"

He shrugged. "I don't worry about things that didn't happen."

Donna looked over the two authors she'd just finished researching. Mac Fortner was another TropicalAuthors writer, songwriter, and veteran. With his Sunny Ray and Cam Derringer series having nine books published between them and another one on the horizon, he could hardly have been as retired as he claimed. Songwriting was something that intrigued her. It might be interesting to Sanford as well.

Steve Kittner was new to TA, but not to the publishing world. Interestingly enough, he started writing adventure stories about his native West Virginia, but switched locations mid-series to Florida's Treasure Coast, and finally to the Keys. His "What Lies" adventure mystery series was now comprised of four books, but in the middle of it he also wrote a children's book to be used as a tool for teaching kids the importance of carrying out their chores around the house. From what she'd seen of this younger generation he'd have been better off spending that time writing a book about herding cats.

Not only was the "What Lies" series's almost thousand-mile location change unusual, but so was his three-year gap between books three and four. Especially since he had plenty of high ratings and reviews for the series. She made a mental note to ask him about that when she met him.

She had four more writers to research but decided to go over to the *Cape Charles Coffee House* for a late breakfast first. It was only a five-minute walk from the e-b&b garage apartment that she'd rented for the week. The morning was crystal clear, the temperature moderate and perfect for her walk. Along the way she picked up today's *ESVA Telegraph*, folding it in half, intending to read it with her breakfast.

Donna didn't know what it was about this server, she had been the one who first waited on her when she'd arrived in Cape Charles. She'd acted very standoffish and almost nervous around her ever since. Some people can be so sensitive, she mused. The server took her order and then brought her coffee. As Donna took her first sip, she unfolded the *Telegraph* and almost spewed her coffee all over it. There on the front page was the picture of a large fish and a group of people standing around it, including Sanford! And that young writer, Micah Monroe, was standing right beside him. To top it all off, the picture was taken yesterday at *Mallard Cove Marina*, that place she had stayed the first night she'd gotten here.

So, Sanford *was* already here on ESVA and apparently, he knew this Micah person. She wondered just how well he knew her. As pretty and young as she was, it would be easy for her to sidle up to a gentleman of Sanford's age, and prey on him. Well, she wasn't about to let that happen, or happen any further if it already had. And it looked like it might've. No doubt she was using him for publicity like this picture to advance her writing career.

She studied the picture and saw they were posed in front of a fishing boat named *Predator*, and its hailing port was someplace named *Bayside, VA*. So, she now had two clues as to where Sanford might be keeping his boat. She read the caption and saw the fish was a yellowfin tuna, and citation size, whatever that meant. It had been landed by Elaina Clarke, the daughter of Eric Clarke, who was standing next to her. Also pictured was the boat owner, Casey Shaw, along with Betsy Riggins, famed novelist Sandy Morgan, coastal adventure writer Micah Monroe, and *Predator's* captain, Jeff Smith.

The idiot reporter must have missed that his name was *Sanford*, not Sandy. It also went on to say that Eric Clarke and Casey Shaw were business partners with stakes in *Mallard Cove, Bayside Resort and Marina*, the *Bluffs Restaurant and Marina*, as well as a new marina development under construction in Cape Charles and several other properties beyond ESVA.

Well, she already knew that Sanford's boat wasn't here. But since he was obviously friends with both Shaw and Clarke, it made sense that he might dock it at any of those other three marinas they owned. First things first, she would have her breakfast. Then she would go back to *Mallard Cove* and hunt for Sanford's boat and that sport-fishing boat, *Predator*. If he wasn't there, that boat's crew could probably tell her where he was. If she couldn't find that one either, she'd move on to *The Bluffs* and then, if necessary, *Bayside*. One way or another, she would find Sanford. Today. She could barely contain her excitement.

The server delivered her breakfast, and Donna grabbed her by the arm, shoving the picture in front of her. "See? I told you he was here! *This* is Sanford Morgan, my close friend, and he's somewhere around here. I know where *Mallard Cove* is, but what about *Bayside* and the *Bluffs Marina*? I need to get to both of those!"

The server was freaked out to have this crazy woman grab her arm and she yanked it away. "Those are both north of here, up in Accomack County. You'll have to ask for directions up there." She hurried away from this nightmare customer, silently hoping she would never come back in again.

The most scenic way to see many of the best parts of ESVA was by boat. For that reason, Sandy and Betsy have now headed out again in her center console outboard, on their way to Cape Charles. Micah had been concerned when she heard about their destination, but Sandy assured her that they'd be fine.

"When that woman couldn't find me up there, she probably moved on. It's likely to be the safest place for me in Virginia right now. Besides, if you haven't heard, I have a very hard head. If she tries to hit me, she'll just hurt her hand." He laughed, both at his joke about his head and the absurdity of the whole situation.

Micah pulled up the picture of the "clinger" and showed it to Betsy before sending it to Sandy's phone. "That's what she looks like.

Both of you please keep an eye out for her, okay? She was very insistent, and not very lucid."

Sandy smiled and looked at Betsy, "Lucid. She uses all those writer words now."

"Yes, lucid! And I've been using that word in conversation since long before I ever started writing. Sheesh!"

"Not to worry, we're both still *lucid* enough to spot a lunatic a mile away, and we can handle ourselves." Sandy used his fingers as air quotes around "lucid enough."

Micah sighed, "It's my job to worry about you."

"Consider this your day off. Betsy, you're officially in charge of worrying about me today."

"Oh, no! Don't drag me into this fight."

Sandy said, "This isn't a fight, it's a slight disagreement. She worries too much, and I want her to relax."

With that, they climbed into Betsy's outboard and cast off. Their trip up the smooth-surfaced Chesapeake was relaxing, a stark contrast to yesterday's washing machine ride offshore in the Atlantic. Since they weren't fishing today, Betsy had slowed the boat to a fast cruise, much to Sandy's relief. Less than half an hour later they pulled into the harbor at Cape Charles. After they tied up at the marina, they cut through the rail yard property that Casey's group was in the process of developing on Mason Street, the main drag. Since it was Sunday, most of the quaint little shops on the street wouldn't open for another half hour. So, they headed for the coffee shop to kill some time over another cup. The server came over to their table and did a double-take. She looked nervous.

"Are you Sanford Morgan?"

"Sandy, but yes."

"A friend of yours was in here a couple of times, looking for you."

Sandy took out his phone and showed her the picture of the mystery woman. The server nodded. "That's her. She was in here a while ago and got all excited when she saw your picture in the paper with that tuna."

Sandy sighed, "She's not a friend. I've never even met her. Not anxious to, either."

"In that case, you should know she tore out of here a little while ago to try and find you. She said she knew where *Mallard Cove* was but wanted directions to *Bayside* and *The Bluffs*."

Sandy looked at Betsy, "Well, that ought to keep her busy the rest of today, and we can enjoy Cape Charles without running into her."

"You probably should give Micah a 'heads up' though," Betsy suggested.

"Not a bad idea. I'll text her." He turned back to the server, "Thanks so much for the warning. If she comes back in, I'd appreciate it if you wouldn't tell her we were here."

"Not a problem. And nothing personal, but I hope she never comes back. She gives me the creeps."

"You're not alone in that," Betsy said.

Micah was on her way over to Lindsay's houseboat when she read the text and then shared it with her when she got there. Lindsay began texting, and by the time she was finished, a special reception had been arranged for the mystery woman at all three venues she planned on visiting.

10 DON'T PASS "GO"

Donna parked next to *Mallard Cove's* charter boat row and then began canvassing the docks, looking for Sanford's boat or that *Predator* fishing boat. She was three-quarters of the way through when she was approached by a large, imposing man with a Bahamian accent.

"You look like you be lost. Can I help you with sometin'? I'm Barry, de dockmaster."

"Yes! I'm looking for either Sanford Morgan's boat or that fishing boat named *Predator.*"

"An' you are…?"

"I'm a close, personal friend of Mr. Morgan's, and I must find him."

"Oh, I see. What is his boat name, an' is he expectin' you?"

"So, you know him? He was here last night with that big fish." She was excited to finally be making progress.

"Sorry, I can't comment 'bout boat owners or dere guests without dere permission."

"As I said, I'm a very close friend of his, and he would tell you that it's perfectly fine to give me the information that I need."

"Since he's not here, I can't confirm dat. An' access to our docks is limited to de boat owners and dere guests, so now you got to leave."

"I *am* his guest; don't you understand that! I just need to know where his boat is."

"De boat dat you don' even know de name of. Miss, it's time you gotta go."

"I told you, we're *friends*."

"I given you two chances, now I'm gwan to call de sheriff."

As he took his cell phone out of his pocket, she slapped it out of his hand and it sailed down the dock, almost going over the edge and into the water. Usually as gentle as a teddy bear, Barry became someone you didn't want to mess with when he was mad, and Donna had just crossed that line. She immediately realized her mistake and took off running down the dock, heading in the direction of the *Cove* and the beach bars. Barry picked up his phone which fortunately hadn't been damaged and hit a speed dial number.

"Mimi? She's here an' headed your way. She jus' slapped de phone outta my han'. Dis one's crazy."

"Got it, Barry, thanks. Should we call the sheriff? You want to press charges?"

"No, nuthin' like dat. We jus' need to scare her outta here so she don' come back."

"Got it, thanks." She ducked into the kitchen and came back out with two of the larger staff members just as Donna walked up to the service bar, asking about Sandy. They approached her from behind, and Mimi tapped her on the shoulder. "Ma'am, I'm going to have to ask you to leave."

Donna turned and said, "I'm looking for my friend, Sanford Morgan. He was here last night, and he doesn't know how to get in touch with me. I must find him."

"You need to go somewhere else to try and find him because you've been told to leave by the dockmaster and now by me, so that means you're trespassing."

"You don't get it; I'll leave when I'm ready. I need to know if anyone here has seen him today." She started to turn back toward the bar, but Mimi put a restraining hand on her shoulder. Donna spun back around, this time balling up her fists.

Mimi said, "You really don't want to do that. You need to get in your car and leave while you can still walk out of here, or you'll spend the next thirty days as a guest of the county."

Ordinarily, Donna wouldn't have backed down. She believed she had every right to be there, that Sanford would want her there, but the idea of missing out on the cruise with him while she sat in jail terrified her. Not only would she literally miss the boat, but the cops would find out who she was, and she couldn't afford that. She glared at Mimi and went out through the front door, circling the building and going back to her car.

Sitting in the car while looking out over the marina, she still didn't spot *Predator* or any boat that looked like it could be Sanford's. What she did see however was that guy Barry who was now double-timing it in her direction. She backed out of her spot and spun her tires as she shot through the parking lot. Taking a right as she reached the main road, she headed for the next closest place where Sanford might be staying, *The Bluffs Marina*.

She thought *The Bluffs* looked nice; it had new floating docks and a long, tiki-style thatched roof bar attached to the restaurant. But it was like they had been expecting her, from the crews of the commercial boats on the docks to those sitting up at the bar. They all were unco-operative at first, and then became openly hostile when she didn't back down. Hostile enough that she ended up almost running back to her car. Then a ratty old pickup truck with an equally ratty-looking driver pulled in behind her as she left. He followed her out of the parking lot and back to the main road, at one point less than a foot from her bumper. She got the message and was never going back. There was no way she would ever believe that Sanford would have anything to do with those people anyway.

Ten minutes later Donna pulled in through the front entrance of *Bayside Resort and Marina*. Beautifully manicured flower beds lined the long asphalt driveway. Halfway down the drive, another driveway led off to the right where an imposing-looking wrought iron electric gate blocked public access. A fancy black sign with gold leaf lettering declared it to be the private owners' entrance to *Bayside Estates*. Strategically placed foliage shielded any prying eyes from seeing what lay beyond.

Driving in farther she saw a marina ahead with an open-air beach café on the shore of the Chesapeake, a boutique-style three-story hotel to the right of that, and a nondescript one-story office building on the other side of its circular drive. All had the same Nantucket style with faux cedar shingles and green metal roofing. Another driveway intersected the circle, paralleling the Chesapeake, with rental cottages between it and the water. The road continued past the cottages but was blocked by another imposing gate, this one controlled by a guard that was stationed in a small building off to the side. Another of those black and gold signs announced that the *Bayside Club and Spa*, and *Bayside Estates and Marina* lay beyond, but that access was limited to members, owners, and their guests.

This had the right feel to it and was the kind of place where Sanford would live. Maybe that picture of him on the boat was just a publicity shot, staged to make people believe that he lived aboard. Perhaps instead he had one of the homes back in the private estates. She could visualize him living there, with her at his side, of course.

She suddenly realized that she had stopped her car, and another had pulled up behind her. The driver impatiently drove around her, shooting her an irritated look as he passed. She decided to look at the public marina and beach café first before she went back into the *Estates*. Maybe someone here could tell her exactly which house was his.

From the seawall on the edge of the marina basin, she looked across the entire marina. This included the far side which was also private, secured by another security fence and gate. She didn't see either *Predator* or a boat that would've matched the picture of the one in the book. But that wasn't a surprise. *Predator* was no doubt tucked away in that other even more exclusive marina at the *Estates*. Her doubts about Sanford living on a boat had grown stronger. That Shaw fellow probably had an estate home here, and it was likely that Sanford was his neighbor.

Donna walked over to the café's patio, picking out a table facing the beach. It might have been her imagination, but she thought she saw glimpses of recognition on the faces of the two servers and the bartender. But why? Maybe after she was with Sanford and they were frequently photographed together this would be a common occurrence, but as far as she knew the only photos of her were...

"Can I help you?" The server had an almost chilly tone, not welcoming at all, and she wasn't even offering to show Donna a menu.

Ignoring her tone, Donna said, "I'll take a cup of coffee."

"We're out of coffee."

"Fine, I can get a cup at my friend's home, Sanford Morgan. Which of the places in the *Estates* is his? I've forgotten."

"It's our policy not to give out information about any of our residents." Delivered without an apology, and in a very brusque manner.

Bingo, she thought, the woman said "residents." Her hunch had been correct, Sanford has a house here. "And of course, you shouldn't, at least not to the public. But I'm a close personal friend of his. I just missed him down in Islamorada, and I need to catch up with him here."

"Then maybe you should call him and make sure he's home."

"I've lost his number."

"Sounds like you're out of luck."

Donna was getting mad, "I don't like your attitude."

"And I don't like getting lied to. In fact, you should leave."

"I want to see the manager."

"That would be me."

"What kind of an outfit would hire someone so ill-equipped to deal with customers as you?"

"Again, you need to leave. Now. Or I can have the sheriff escort you off the property."

Donna stood up and glared at the woman, "I'm going to tell Sanford about how rudely I was treated here, and he'll be glad to pass that along to your boss. They're fishing buddies you know."

"Yes, I do know that. As does anyone who read the *ESVA Telegraph* this morning. Now leave."

Without another word, Donna stormed out. She felt like dozens of eyes were on her as she walked to her car. The place which had felt so welcoming when she first arrived now felt hostile to her. At least the public side of it. Maybe she would have better luck on the private side. She drove over to the *Estates* guard shack and rolled down the window as the guard stepped out and held up an open palm.

"Hi. I'm Fawn Liebowitz, I'm here to see Sanford Morgan."

The guard smiled faintly and said, "Nice try. But everyone knows that 'Fawn' died in a kiln explosion in that Animal House movie. And the café manager has already called about you. So, you need to turn around and exit the grounds, since you've already been told that you're trespassing."

"I'm not trespassing, I'm here to see my friend, and he's not going to be happy when I tell him how I've been treated."

"Last chance, lady. Turn around now and leave or wait for the cops, it's up to you."

She frowned then burned rubber in reverse just to show how irritated she was. She sped down the center of the long driveway on her way out, running one incoming guest's car off the pavement. Now furious at what she recognized as a coordinated strategy to run her off by people who wanted to isolate Sanford and keep her away from him.

Well, they might get away with this here on land, but she already had her cabin bought and paid for on the cruise, and Sanford would be furious when she told him all about it. They couldn't keep her away from him on that ship.

$\sim$

Cape Charles had been a fun run for the two of them. Great shopping in small independent stores, a walk on the beach, followed up by a fantastic lunch in an old bank building. Their table was in what had originally been the vault. A couple of Bloody Marys each with lunch, and then a "flight" of sample shots at a distillery's tasting room across the street. Sandy now knew what Casey saw in their vodka; it was his favorite brand. It was like drinking sweet rainwater, but with a kick like a mule. Despite being more of a beer guy, he bought several bottles, as did Betsy.

On the ride back to *Mallard Cove*, a very happy and relaxed Betsy relinquished the helm to Sandy. He made a mental note to start the search for an outboard of his own after he got back from the cruise. He missed the freedom that came with running a smaller boat by himself, without needing help from anyone else like he did with *Epilogue*. While he'd been handling the dock lines today for Betsy, this was only because it was easier with two people. Each of them was perfectly capable of handling this boat solo.

After successfully avoiding Sandy's stalker all day, the two of them decided to switch their grilling venue from *Cheri* over to the more private *C2*. Lindsay had called Sandy with an update on the woman's movements and actions. They all agreed that she would probably disappear now that she had been run off from all three properties. They knew that any face-to-face meeting with Sandy would likely end up being unpleasant. Not wanting to ruin what had otherwise been a perfect day, moving over to the pool deck didn't seem like a bad alternative.

11 FUTURE PLANS

Over in the clubhouse at *C2*, Sandy made a pitcher of spicy Bloody Marys, with a generous helping of Cape Charles vodka. Hearing an approaching helicopter, he doubled up on everything and grabbed extra glasses, putting them all on a tray. He joined Betsy on the pool deck just as Eric, Candi, Missy, Casey, and Dawn arrived, with big grins on all their faces. The adults quickly helped themselves to Sandy's concoction, since all alcohol at *C2* was considered fair game.

"I take it this is one of the two best days in the life of a boat owner. And since you didn't go down there to sell one, I'm guessing you bought your hull," Sandy said.

Eric replied, "Worked out a fair deal, got a verbal agreement from the original owner, and they'll get back working on it this week after everything gets put down on paper. And it's a lot further along than just a hull."

"She, Dad, or her, not 'it,'" Missy corrected her father. "Sandy, you should see her lines, she's beautiful! The cockpit seems twice as large, but in all the right places. She's going to be a dream to fish. If you thought *Steel Leader* looked like a great fishing platform, wait until you see *Sharke*."

Betsy said, "*Sharke*? Not another *Predator*?"

"No, *Predator* is still our boat. *Sharke* with a silent 'e' at the end is our partnership boat. The name is a combination of Shaw and Clarke," Dawn said.

Sandy remarked, "Clever. And since you all agreed so well and so fast on the name, maybe this partnership thing has a chance of making it after all."

Missy showed Sandy and Betsy a four-minute video walk-through of the boat she had filmed and stored on her tablet. When it got to the engine room, Sandy whistled.

"What beasts for engines! And I guess the big drum-looking thing in the middle is that Furuno sonar. I can see why you said it would be tight squeezing one into *Predator*, Casey. Nice that this room was designed from the start for one." Sandy was impressed.

"For the Seakeeper, too. Plus, twin generators. Checks off all the boxes for everything I want in a new rig. I'm anxious to see that Furuno in action though. They said *Steel Leader* is working her way up north, and they're going to see if they can arrange to have her stop by here on the way back. Then we can get a demo ride and see exactly how that new sonar works," Casey said.

"Here's to a smooth, fast ride," Sandy raised his glass, followed by everyone else.

Donna was still seething when she got back to the garage apartment. Somehow, someone was coordinating an effort to keep her away from Sanford. If she didn't know better, she'd swear it started with that bitch Sanford sold his store to. Could she have called the security office at *Bayside Estates*, and they put out the word throughout that company's properties? He was tied in with the owners, and they might have an interest in protecting him. If they only understood she wanted the same thing for him. Even though she'd been blocked from seeing Sanford so far, she appreciated how careful they were to protect him. Almost as careful as she would be at preserving his privacy when she was finally with him.

And while their security was good, if that cretin who followed her out of *The Bluffs* was part of their team, they had stooped low when they hired him. So far, they must not have identified her since they referred to her as "Miss" and "lady." If they only knew who she was, and what she'd had to do to finally make this trip, well, things might've gotten a lot more... dicey.

Eric, Candi, and Missy left in the helicopter about an hour before dark, headed back to the building in Northern Virginia that served as both Eric's corporate headquarters and their home. Casey and Dawn went back to their boat soon after they left, having full calendars themselves tomorrow morning.

Betsy said, "I don't know about you, but I've had about all the tomato juice I can handle. You know, vodka on the rocks goes well with grilled tuna."

"We can switch over, no problem."

"You know, for a guy who so highly covets his beer, you certainly are liberal with your new vodka, making all those Bloody Marys for everyone earlier."

"Because it wasn't beer; there's a difference. People tend to drink less of my booze than they do beer. And a bottle of vodka weighs a lot less than a case of beer when you have to lug it home."

She shook her head slightly, "Maybe it's the vodka, but somehow that seems to make sense, in a warped kind of way."

"The more vodka you drink, the more sense it makes."

"The more vodka I drink, the happier I am to be here with you."

He grinned, "I think we have some taller glasses around here somewhere."

Donna was now back at her research, continuing to build the dossier. According to the list in the email that announced the cruise, there were four left that she hadn't dug into yet.

Brian (B.R.) Spangler. A writer of crime thrillers, science fiction, horror stories, paranormal and contemporary fiction. Over a dozen so far with the most recent ones being set on the Outer Banks of North Carolina. Interesting, Donna thought, another coastal writer who started early on by writing poetry and songs. Sanford might enjoy talking with him since he also lived in Virginia; they now had that in common.

Bryan Peabody was kind of an enigma. He had one published book in his Caribbean Mystery Series, and another that was set to launch, both centered around his character, Conner Cole. Living somewhere in the southeast, he loved traveling to new islands in the Caribbean, and new locations in South America. If she was going to find out more about him, that would have to happen aboard ship.

Axel Blackwell. Now here was a writer whose life read like it was straight from the pages of a book. A liveaboard "in an old trawler on a misty bay on the northwest edge of America." He claimed to have been "a preacher man, a salesman, and a lawman." And now a writer with nine published books, three of which were a series co-written by one of the biggest independent coastal writers in the business. His two stand-alone novels were paranormal thrillers, completely different from the two series. He had a nice ability to cross between genres. Sanford might find a lot of value in chatting with him about the Pacific Northwest, something she planned to suggest. And up until she discovered that Sanford now made his home at *Bayside Estates* instead of on a boat, she'd have told him about the two of them having that in common.

The last writer on the list was Doug Brisotti. He bounced around from Long Island to Florida, and finally ended up in coastal North Carolina. He had one stand-alone book, and a series of coastal action books about a guy who lived aboard a Hatteras boat in Dare County, North Carolina. As art often imitated life, Brisotti also lived aboard his own Hatteras in Beaufort and chartered it when he wasn't writing or working in the media business.

She decided to hunker down here in this apartment until it was time to head to Norfolk and board the ship. Going back to *Bayside* would be too risky; she couldn't afford a run-in with the law, just in case. Probably nobody had figured it all out but there was no sense tempting the Fates. Instead, she would make use of the time committing all this information to memory, especially their photos, and reading at least one book from each. She wanted to be able to converse intelligently with all of them as soon as they were introduced, something that would undoubtedly impress Sanford.

It seemed like her entire life had been building up to this upcoming event and that one moment. It would be the first time that she and Sanford would be unattached and at the same place at the same time. While it was true that they'd met twice before, the first time was before he'd become a widower. And then last year they'd met again at another book signing in the fall, though she wasn't free, at least not at that point. But now she was. Her husband and son were both gone, liberating her from that boring, ordinary life she'd been living. It had barely been an existence.

No, that wasn't true. Sanford's books had lifted her out of that life, showing her there were places and experiences beyond the repetitive, unending rut that had become her world. She had been desperate to get out; she *deserved* a reprieve from her self-made hell. No, that wasn't true either. She hadn't created it. The continual demands and needs of their farm, her husband, and her son had. They had all been shackled to it, out in the middle of nowhere, with their closest neighbor almost a mile away. Sadly, this had been the life her son had wanted too, just as his father did. She had such high hopes for her boy, that he would achieve so much more. But as far as he was concerned, the world ended at the fence line along their property's edge, and he wanted nothing else. One day he would find a girl who would be willing to move there with him. They would have been shackled together to these same several hundred acres of earth. It would've sucked the soul out of both of them, just as it had her now-dead husband, and as it had threatened to do to her.

But Sanford's books had changed all that. They had been a window into an exciting life on the coast, expressed through his many stories. She didn't just read his books, she immersed herself in them, and they became a part of her. Donna was able to see with total clarity all the qualities of this great writer through his words. Gradually the realization had hit her; they were soulmates, meant to be together. But she figured for that to happen she first needed to be free. She decided she would also free her husband and son. Which meant she would also be saving the life of some young woman not unlike herself. Someone who would have lost her soul as well to that patch of dust and dirt, just like she had come close to forever losing hers.

"That pool looks awfully inviting, Sandy," Betsy said. It was dark now, the underwater pool light providing the only illumination in the area.

He nodded, "Well, I guess we can run back to our boats and change into our trunks."

She put her arms around his neck. "I don't know if it's you, the vodka, or a combination of both, but I'm willing to skip that step if you are. It's been years since I've been skinny-dipping, and this feels like the perfect place and the perfect time to break that streak."

He grinned, "You might be right about that."

"Trust me, I am."

12 PAST HISTORY

Six months earlier, and several states away...

Her timing had been perfect; Donna was going to make her usual shopping trip to the nearest big city, some sixty miles away. Not coincidentally the city's largest bookstore just happened to be hosting a book signing that day for Sanford's latest book. She'd planned this well. As per usual she would leave around dawn. This would get her to the warehouse club store where they usually shopped, at around its opening time. Only this morning she wasn't loading up on everything at once, only the nonperishables. She wanted the time stamp on the receipt to prove she had been over an hour away from the farm as her son and husband had drifted off peacefully into that forever sleep. Their life sentences in that agricultural prison would now be fully pardoned. Then her husband's life insurance would be enough for her to retire the bank's note on the farm, then she could barely wait to sell it.

Anticipating seeing Sanford this morning bolstered her confidence. Not that she could change anything by that time anyway. Creatures of habit, her husband and son started their days around sunup in the small office of the farm's maintenance shop, setting their plans before they headed out into the fields. But on this day, so soon after harvest, they planned on working all day in the shop and took their time getting over there. They normally did their annual maintenance on the equipment in the warm comfort of that building through the winter months. The shop had been constructed ten years ago, back when soybean profits peaked at more than double where they were today. They barely broke even now, and the future outlook was dismal. Back then though they could afford to have the new shop built strong and fully weatherproof, able to stand up to the area's harsh winter winds. This was a quality building with a good furnace. A propane furnace.

The night before, Donna cleaned up the kitchen after dinner as usual. But then she slipped out the back door and walked over to the empty shop. Once inside she started a tractor that was in front of the furnace, located at the far end of the building. She backed it into the unit and shoved it until the stack began to separate from the exhaust vent. Then she parked the tractor back in its original position, several feet away from it. From that point on, every time the furnace fired it would expel carbon monoxide gas into the building. By the time the two men got to work the next morning most of the oxygen would have been displaced. Being colorless and odorless they wouldn't notice the lack of oxygen, or if they did, by then it would be too late for them to get back out before being overcome by hypoxia.

After loading up at the warehouse club she made several more stops in the city, including of course the bookstore. When she first spotted Sanford, it was like an electric current was shooting through her. For the first time in years, she felt fully alive. When he glanced at her, giving her a look of stealthy recognition, she almost swooned. It made everything she'd done, everything she'd gone through, all worthwhile. Time stood still as he signed her book and then handed it to her, almost smiling as he did. So elated, that she didn't even remember walking back to the truck. She didn't want to leave, but she couldn't afford to have him in any way connected to her. For now.

A few more stores to go, and then her final stop was back once again at the warehouse club. This time it was for the dairy and cold items she hadn't wanted to pick up earlier and have to leave in the truck all day. After that she headed back to the farm, dreading being the one to discover the bodies. As it turned out though, that dread was interest on a debt she wouldn't have to pay. As she turned into her long gravel driveway she spotted numerous sheriff's cars, a van, and a delivery truck parked outside of the shop. An unlucky guy from the tractor supply store had been delivering a parts order when he discovered the lifeless men, and barely made it back outside before being overcome himself.

Donna put on a tremendous performance for everyone there, leaving little doubt in anyone's mind that she was the grieving widow and mother. At least in *most* of their minds.

Rookie Deputy Carl Linton felt there was something off about how the widow was acting; things might not be as they seemed on the surface. He started looking through her truck, discovering a signed copy of a Sanford Morgan book on the front seat, the inscription wishing her "all the best." But the way the groceries and supplies were placed in the back seat of the crew cab bothered him. He couldn't put his finger on why, but something was subconsciously nagging him about it. Out of habit, he took a picture of their placement, as well as one of a time-stamped club store receipt he spotted.

Every outward indication was that the two men had died as the result of a terrible accident. One of them must've backed a tractor in too far the night before, its huge back tires shoving the furnace back just enough to break it loose from the exhaust stack. A black tire mark was still visible there on the unit's now dented sheet metal front cover.

Maybe that was part of what was bothering him. This shop building was around a decade old, but you could eat off the floor, it was kept that clean. Their tools had all been wiped down before being put away. Clearly, farming had been their lives, but the deputy couldn't recall seeing any other farm where the equipment had been steam cleaned at the end of the season before being brought into the shop for maintenance. The tractor that had struck the furnace was an older one, yet it too was spotless and showed evidence of having had its paint touched up through the years. So many farmers didn't care if their equipment was rusty, greasy, and caked with dirt, so long as each one started and did their job each season. They didn't spend money and time on things like paint. But not these two men who were so meticulous about everything they did. So why would one of them not take the time to look over the furnace after he backed into it? A cursory inspection would have quickly revealed that loose stack behind it. This just seemed out of character for them both; the way they lived and worked. Ironically, deviating from this became the reason they died.

Another thing that bothered him was the way the widow kept stealing glances at him when she thought he wasn't looking. In those brief moments, her face looked more worried and even scared than it was grief-stricken. But worried or scared about what? There was no outward indication of foul play. And according to that warehouse club receipt he'd just found in her truck, she had started her day early over in the city. She hadn't been near here when the men went into the shop. Of course, that didn't mean she couldn't have set this in motion before she left, or after they were done for the day yesterday.

"Linton! What the hell are you doing?" The sheriff had walked up behind him as he stood at the truck's open door.

Keeping his voice low he replied, "Something is bothering me about this, Sheriff. I'm just searching to see..."

"Searching without any probable cause! You want to tell me what it is that's bugging you? Enough to come over here and violate the rights of a woman who just lost her entire family? Tell me, how many bodies have you seen since you started in my department?"

"Um, these are my first two."

"Un huh. I'm gonna let you in on a secret they didn't tell you in your training class. Not every body you'll see in this county is the result of a homicide. We haven't had a homicide since those two migrant workers did a slice and dice on each other three years ago. Son, I know that things must seem boring now that you've completed your training and have a couple of months of patrol under your belt.

But that's how it is around here, and frankly, I like it like that. So, I don't want you going around upsetting that poor woman, she's been through enough today. How's about giving the coroner a hand loading the deceased into his van and giving your conspiracy theories a rest? Oh, and pick that up," he motioned to an errant piece of paper that had fallen out of the truck. "This place is neat as a pin, and I don't want people thinking that any of us were littering."

Throughout the sheriff's dressing-down, the deputy had felt heat rising in his cheeks. He was thankful for the chance to bend down and look away.

After helping the coroner like he'd been told, he got back into his car and followed the van down the driveway, in a hurry to get back out on patrol. The sheriff and an older deputy were busy talking to the widow, and he wanted to make himself scarce. Back out on the road, he was happy to be alone with his thoughts. That's when he realized what had been bothering him about the way the truck was loaded; the cold and frozen items had all come from the same warehouse club as the nonperishables. The store that she had checked out of early this morning. The temperature was cool, but not cool enough to have left those items sitting out in the truck all day. They were separated from the nonperishable items by a pile of supplies from other stores. And, come to think of it, none of the cold items had appeared on the receipt. Meaning, she must've gone back. Why hadn't she bought everything there at once while on her way home?

Suddenly his thoughts were interrupted by a radio call about an armed robbery in progress at the county's only gas and convenience station, a business that coincidentally was owned by the sheriff's sister and brother-in-law. Pondering over the widow's grocery shopping timetable would have to wait as now he was focused on what might be in store for him ahead. It had been called in by a customer who had seen what was happening and had fled. The store was situated by itself on a rural two-lane road, a lone outpost, perfect for robbing.

Two minutes later he pulled up in front of the store. As he exited his vehicle the store's front door opened. A wild-eyed tweaker was coming out of the store, using the sheriff's sister as a shield, holding her by her hair. The woman was hysterical, and the tweaker was coming down off his latest methamphetamine high. The combination of the two wasn't good. Neither was the fact there was a cheap revolver in the tweaker's hand, which now alternated between being pointed at his hostage's head and Deputy Linton. He was dragging the woman toward a battered, sad-looking older sedan.

The deputy knew he couldn't let him get her into the car or she would be as good as dead. He tried talking to him, but it only enraged the addict, who was clearly out of it. He brought the gun to bear again on Linton just as the lawman saw he had a clear shot at the man's head. They both fired simultaneously, and the last thing the deputy recalled seeing was the red and gray mist that blew out of the back of the man's head. Then a sledgehammer hit him in the chest, and his world went black.

"Hey, son, you back with us?"

The deputy opened his eyes and saw a concerned-looking sheriff bending over him. He struggled to remember where he was... it was a gas station, right? But this looked like it was the inside of a very bright room.

"Sheriff?"

"You rest easy, son; you've been unconscious for a bunch of days. You did good, saving my sister like you did."

"The robber..."

"You gave him what he had comin' to him. No judge, no jury, only old-fashioned nine-millimeter justice. But don't you worry about a thing, just rest up. You gave us quite a scare; it was nip and tuck there for a while. But Doc says you're on the mend, and you'll be out of here and back home in a week or so. Then you'll be at a desk back at the office in a month or two; light duty at first you know. But rest up for now. Oh, and I'm personally gonna buy you a bulletproof vest. You ain't going out again without it."

The sheriff's timetable proved to be correct; it was almost two months later before Deputy Linton was back in uniform. The bullet had almost killed him, and it had been a long, tough road back. His old uniform was ruined by the bullet hole and the large pool of blood he had lain in, not to mention the ER nurse's scissors after he got to the hospital.

In his locker, he had found a brand-new uniform hanging in its place, also purchased by the sheriff. A sealed evidence bag loaded with what had been in his pockets on that fateful day had been waiting on the locker's shelf. Included in the bag was a slip of paper; he remembered it was the one the sheriff had him pick up out at the farm. At this point, he almost threw it out but glanced at it instead. Suddenly his original suspicions came flooding back. It was the receipt for Donna DuBois's cold items, purchased at that same warehouse club store, and time-stamped almost seven hours after her first stop there that morning.

There was something else about the receipt that stuck out to him. The warehouse club's computer register system had printed a note on the receipt reminding her that a prescription refill for Jack DuBois was ready and waiting at the pharmacy. He pulled out his phone and looked at the picture of the other receipt he'd taken that day. It had the same reminder printed on it.

So, Donna DuBois ignored not just one but two reminders that day to pick up a prescription refill for her husband. She had said that it was her usual every second week's run over to the city for supplies. So, why wouldn't she have picked up his prescription, especially since by the time she returned in two weeks, the pharmacy would've returned it to their shelves? He wondered if maybe she hadn't had enough money, but after looking over both receipts, there were several frivolous items that could've been omitted to free up enough cash for the prescription.

He called the pharmacy, running into the usual "patient confidentiality" issues until he explained that the person he was inquiring about was deceased and that this was a suspicious death investigation. While the pharmacist wouldn't reveal exactly which drug this was, she did say that it hadn't been picked up on that date or any subsequent day, and it was one that you couldn't stop "cold turkey." If you quit taking it, you'd need to be weaned off it under a doctor's supervision, and it wasn't that expensive. It made no sense unless she had known her husband wasn't going to need the refill because he was going to be dead.

"Good to see you back in uniform, son." The sheriff had walked in, startling him.

"Thank you, sir. I've found something interesting in that DuBois case."

The sheriff frowned, recalling that he'd told the young deputy to stop investigating it. But the boy had taken a bullet while saving his only sister, so he was bound to have to give him more latitude. "Okay, what've you got?"

When Linton laid out what he had found, the sheriff seemed lost in thought for a moment. Then he said, "Okay since you're gonna be flyin' a desk for a little while anyway, I guess it won't hurt to look into things a little further. Lemme know what ya find."

Two hours later the deputy walked into the sheriff's office. "Sir? I think you need to see this." He handed the sheriff a fax from a police department in a neighboring state. It was a report of a suspected homicide from over two decades ago. The victim had been a young male who was found dead of carbon monoxide poisoning in his garage, his car left running inside. But the medical examiner had discovered he had been knocked unconscious first before being placed in the car, so it was ruled a homicide rather than suicide. No one was ever charged. Several people were questioned, including the young man's live-in girlfriend. She was the sole beneficiary of his life insurance policy.

"I talked to the detective who had been assigned to the case, and he said that while they couldn't get enough evidence to charge the woman, he was certain she was good for it. As soon as the insurance company paid off, she disappeared, leaving everything in their rented house."

The sheriff looked annoyed, "So, what has this got to do with anything?"

"Because three months later she married Jack DuBois."

"You're sure she's the same woman?"

"Positive."

"I know you're supposed to be on desk duty, but do you feel up to taking a car ride with me?"

"Yes, sir!"

As they pulled into the driveway, they could see a box truck backed in by the side door of the house. The sheriff recognized the man standing beside it as the neighboring farm owner.

"Hey Floyd, what are you doing here?"

"Bought the place, Sheriff. Donna DuBois made me a heck of a deal, and I wanted to add her acreage to mine. Changing out some of the furniture though for my boy to move in here."

The deputy asked, "It came furnished?"

Floyd nodded. "She left everything, right down to the food in the fridge, and the forks in the drawer."

"Where's she at now," the sheriff asked.

"She took off, said she wanted a new start somewhere new the hell and gone away from here. Can't say as I blame her after what happened. I bought the place last month. She was gonna use her insurance to pay the place off and then sell it, but I wanted to make sure I didn't lose it, so we went ahead and closed on it, paying off the note as part of it. I let her stay on for free as part of the deal until her insurance paid out. She got her money and took off last Friday."

"Any idea where?"

"Nope. I got the feelin' she didn't want anybody knowin'."

"Thanks, Floyd. Good luck with the new fields."

Back in the car, Linton asked, "What's our next move?"

"When we get back, I want you to put out a BOLO on her truck, 'wanted for questioning, contact our department.' No sense spooking her, she thinks she got away clean. Truth is, she still might've. What we've got are two very similar cases where she's smack in the middle of 'em. We've got a pile of coincidences and some strange behavior, but that's about it. We got nothin' to prove she rigged the furnace. People have been convicted on less, but not much less."

The truck was found later that week at a used car lot, the owner saying he'd bought it for cash from Donna DuBois. He wanted to work a trade on another vehicle, but she just took the cash and left. It was the last time anyone would see her in the state.

13 TRIP PLANNING

Betsy was startled when she opened her eyes. KC was staring at her, his face just inches away from her own. Then she realized there was an arm across her side, and someone lying close behind her. Memories of last night began to surface, and she smiled. There hadn't been anyone else either during or after Claude. As she started to smile, KC began purring.

"Apparently, he approves," Sandy said.

Her smile got wider. "Well, if I could purr, I would right now as well."

"You did your share of purring last night."

"You're complaining?"

"Nope. Just making an observation."

"Keep your observations, ratings, and any other comments to yourself," she said.

"It's what we writers do; we comment on life."

"This had better not end up in any book."

"My parents raised a gentleman, so no, this won't."

They both noticed a slight movement of the boat as someone boarded, then they heard a noise coming from the galley.

Sandy said, "That's Micah, probably making coffee. You've missed your shot at a clean getaway, without the 'walk of shame.'"

"Sandy, I stopped worrying about things like that more years back than I'd care to count. I'm not ashamed of anything I do anymore. Why would you think I'd be ashamed of having spent the night here with you? Unless you're the one who's worried about it."

"Not me, but now you have to get past Micah."

"Ah, the gatekeeper and guardian from the 'widows with casseroles' brigade. And as I told you a while back, I left all my casseroles back in Florida."

Micah was surprised to hear voices coming from Sandy's stateroom. She knew that he and Betsy had gotten close in a very short time but hadn't realized they'd gotten *that* close. The fact that she almost added a "yet" to the end of that thought was somehow comforting. For the last two years, she'd done her best to protect Sandy from potential gold diggers. But Betsy didn't seem to be one of those, and the change in Sandy these past few days had been a good one. Maybe now her responsibilities would be reduced to only taking care of *Epilogue*, and no longer would she be required to watch over her uncle.

"Good morning, Micah," Betsy said as she climbed the companionway stairs.

"Uh, good morning?"

"It is at that," Sandy said. He was close behind on Betsy's heels.

Feeling a bit awkward, Micah asked, "Coffee? I'm just brewing a pot."

Betsy replied, "Thanks, but I think we're headed over to the *Cove* for breakfast. Then I'll leave your uncle to his writing, at least for a while." She looked back at Sandy, grinning.

"That's the plan." Sandy kissed the back of Micah's head as he passed by, adding softly, "Don't worry."

"I'm not." She smiled, but this was directed at Betsy, not him.

"Did I see Betsy leaving with Sandy a while ago?" Lindsay had stopped by *Epilogue* for coffee with Micah.

"Uh-huh."

"Wow. He moved fast."

"I think they both did, but the important part is they're enjoying each other's company. This is the happiest I can remember him being since before my aunt passed."

"He *has* been a bit less of a... grump lately. No offense."

Micah smiled, "None taken. I'm pretty sure he'd agree with you. Though I think he likes being seen as a bit of a curmudgeon, and Betsy doesn't seem to mind it. She's good for him. And if this ends up being a long-term thing, good for them both. Everybody deserves a second chance at happiness. Only now I'm feeling a bit guilty, taking him away from her for almost a week for that author cruise."

"Well, if whatever they have going on is meant to be, a few days' interruption isn't going to make a difference. And speaking of your being gone, do you have somebody lined up to feed KC? I'll be happy to if you don't."

"That would be great! The way to that cat's heart is definitely through his stomach, so you guys might end up being pals."

As if on cue, KC popped back through the cat door in the aft bulkhead, looking up curiously.

Micah said, "Yes, we're talking about you."

KC rubbed against Lindsay's legs as he walked by, on his way to curl up on the dinette bench. She said, "Looks like we are already on the way there."

Sandy didn't get much writing done the rest of the week as he'd planned, not that he minded. The cruise was set to disembark at six p.m. on Saturday and he and Betsy had a late lunch at the *Catamaran* before he left. Betsy looked out and to the west.

"Looks like it might get bumpy this afternoon," she said.

"They said we can expect a line to come through about the time we shove off." Sandy frowned, "It'll probably dog us as we head offshore. Hopefully, this scow is stabilized, and we don't end up with a few hundred 'Ralph the rail huggers' tossing their cookies all night."

In the warmer months in Virginia, most non-tropical weather comes from the west, typically building well east of the Blue Ridge Mountains as it encounters the moister atmosphere of the Tidewater area. The enhanced storm lines can play heck with the marine traffic both in the Chesapeake as well as far offshore until their energy finally dissipates.

Betsy asked, "Sympathetic seasickness?"

"No, I don't lose my lunch just because somebody else does, I just hate the smell of puke." One of the people at a neighboring table shot Sandy a withering stare. "What? If you don't like what I'm saying, quit listening in on a private conversation." The man turned back to his table companions, obviously still irritated.

"Somebody is in a bad mood," Betsy commented.

"What, me or him?"

"You!"

Sandy sighed. "I was just starting to get settled in here, and now I have to do this thing. Don't say anything to Micah, but I'm not looking forward to being trapped on board a boat where I can't get off and away from all those people for a day and a half in both directions. If this wasn't a favor for her, there's no way in hell I'd be going. Usually, when I do book signings, it takes two hours and then I'm out of there. This is going to be like catching the flu, and not being able to shake it for a week."

"Sandy, it's just a short, four-day cruise, and one day of it onshore in Bermuda. Plus, there's that dinner with the governor of Bermuda."

"Oh, whup de freaking do. Have dinner with a damn politician, just what I want to do. I'd rather attend five cocktail parties in Palm Beach, and you know how much I hate those."

"You mean like the one where we met."

"That was the only good that's ever come from one of those things."

She smiled and reached across for his hand. "Thanks for the compliment."

"It's true. And I hate running off and leaving after just starting to get to know you."

"We've been going pretty fast on that."

"I didn't think you minded."

"If I had, trust me, you'd have known it. But I've kept you from writing, and I feel guilty about that."

"If I had minded, I wouldn't have let you."

"It's only for four days, and Micah is such a doll. I'm glad you're there for her. You'll be back here before you know it. Then I'll keep you to your promise of taking me up to St. Michaels, but only if you get back on your writing schedule."

He nodded, exhaling loudly. "You're as bad as my publisher. What, did she call and bribe you?"

"Hah! Maybe I should branch out into extortion."

"You *do* have the proper leverage."

Gray clouds were approaching as Micah and Sandy pulled into the cruise line's VIP departure terminal parking. They grabbed their bags and hurried across the parking lot. Micah presented their tickets on her phone's screen, and the agent called a man over.

"Mr. Morgan, this is your concierge, Jason. Anything you need, he'll handle it." Jason signaled to a crew member who grabbed their bags. As he welcomed them, he led them up an enclosed gangway just as the first raindrops began hitting the windows.

Sandy glanced at Micah, "A concierge? Do I want to know how much I'm paying for this trip?"

"That depends."

His one eyebrow raised, "On?"

"Whether you want to be able to enjoy yourself or not."

Sandy groaned. "At least you said the cabin has its own bar, right?"

"It does. And our tickets are all-inclusive, which means it's like drinking on the house."

"Except I'm making the mortgage payments on that house."

"Something like that."

They followed Jason through a bulkhead with an elaborate set of double wooden doors marked "VIP Guests Only Beyond This Point." There were a half dozen doors beyond it and a large sitting area at the end with a wall of glass facing out aft, beyond the stern. Their suite was the last one on their left. Entering their private living room, they saw the suite was huge and elaborate. Its bar was well stocked, right down to the Red Stripe beer in the small refrigerator.

"Hey, they got the beer right! Is this your work, Jason?" Sandy was impressed.

"I wish I could take the credit, but no, that was due to Miss Monroe, who contacted us and requested we stock your favorite brand."

"It's much appreciated." Sandy took one and opened the bottle.

Jason said, "You saw the suites are situated in a private area for VIP guests only, and my desk is right next to that entrance."

"Sanctuary, sanctuary," Sandy said, in his best Quasimodo voice. "This may not be so bad after all."

Jason looked offended, "Mr. Morgan, we'll do our utmost to make you comfortable and happy, and if there's anything you need, you have only to call me..."

"Relax, Jason, I wasn't talking about you or your ship. I'm just not sure how four full days of fandom is going to go."

"It's rather structured, sir. First though before we sail, both of you need to complete the electronic Muster Drill using the suite's interactive television. It's required by the Coast Guard. Then, after departure, the writers in your group are having a private 'get to know each other' cocktail hour in the Chesapeake Lounge, after which it will be opened to the rest of the members of your group. With so many writers aboard, there should be plenty of readers to go around for everyone," he smiled. "And the Captain has requested that the two of you join her for dinner this evening at the Chef's Table."

Sandy remarked, "Oh, great, another woman who won't let me run her boat."

Jason looked at him questioningly.

"Private joke there, Jason."

He nodded as if he understood, but his face clearly said he didn't. "Tomorrow, the morning is set aside for book signings and mixing with all the authors and readers. Then after lunch, you're scheduled to do your lecture and discussion."

"How many writers are aboard," Sandy asked.

"Twenty-two, including you both."

"And readers?"

"Around three hundred."

"I'm going to need more beer."

Jason chuckled, "I'll see that it's continually re-stocked, sir."

"That's another thing Jason, quit calling me 'sir.' My name's Sandy. 'Sir' makes me feel older than I am, and that's old enough."

"Yes, si... Sandy."

"Good." He looked at Micah, "Well, let's watch this newsreel thingy and get it over with. Hey Jason, I don't suppose there's any popcorn around?"

"Um, I can check..." he looked concerned.

"Relax, Jason, that was another joke. The beer'll do just fine by itself."

After Jason left to go man his desk and the Muster Drill video concluded, Sandy and Micah walked out on their wide, covered balcony, high on the starboard stern corner. They wanted to watch as the ship pulled away from the pier. The storm was ramping up though as the rain increased and was now moving through in sheets. They had to step back from the rail to avoid getting splattered.

Micah said, "I'm surprised they didn't delay our departure a little bit until this storm passed."

"Then they'd have had to speed up to get back on schedule, which would've burned a lot more fuel. Their corporate office wouldn't be too keen on that idea."

Micah still looked concerned. "You've always said that it's one thing to get caught out in a storm but it's stupid to deliberately head out into one."

"True. But there's a big difference between *Epilogue* and this barge.

We're moving away from the pier and yet we can't even hear or feel the engines. We can barely feel the ship moving. Even on the biggest yachts like Casey and Dawn's you can feel the movement and the power of the engines. But not on this thing, which is the biggest boat I've ever been on. Not that it looks like a boat; it's more like a floating hotel."

Lightning was flashing all around them both onshore and out in the bay. Suddenly their world lit up like a camera flash as a lightning bolt hit somewhere directly above their balcony, and there was an instantaneous and deafening clap of thunder. The air suddenly smelled of ozone.

"That almost hit us! C'mon, Sandy, let's get back inside where it's safe." Micah tugged at his hand that wasn't holding the beer, pulling him back into the suite's sitting room and sliding shut the glass door. "Man, that was close!"

"Too close. But then again, we have these." Sandy grinned as he fingered his gris-gris amulet.

"Don't kid around! We could've been killed."

He smiled, seemingly unfazed by the incident. "I'm sure this isn't the only time this ship has been struck by lightning. You can't have a pile of floating metal that's this big and expect it not to get hit. I bet naval architects even have a 'Lightning 101' course they have to take."

"Yeah, well, I don't want to be their lab assignment."

Sandy saw that Micah was shaking and wanted to get her mind off almost being fried. "Hey, let's go find that Chesapeake Lounge."

"We're not due there for another half hour."

"Okay, we can go back to watching the storm on the balcony. I guess we don't want to be early."

Micah replied, "Wait, I know how much you hate it when people are late, so early's good." She hurried toward the cabin door as Sandy grinned.

14 CHANGE OF PLANS

Donna hadn't realized that she would have to park at a remote lot and take a shuttle over a mile to the cruise terminal. As it was, she ended up on the last shuttle run, being picked up in the pouring rain. She and her baggage were thoroughly soaked before they boarded the van. Being last had its advantages though because the terminal personnel were in a hurry to get all the stragglers on board the ship. The ticket agent quickly accepted her explanation about having booked her spot on the author and reader cruise under her pen name instead of the one on her passport. Apparently, the agent knew something about their group but didn't know who the writers were. That, or he didn't care.

This was the point Donna had been dreading. If she had been wanted by the authorities, chances were this would be when she would've been identified and detained. Instead, she breezed right through and made her way down to her lower cabin amidships. She had quite a bit of time before the first "meet-and-greet" mixer in the Chesapeake Lounge and intended on changing into dry clothes and reviewing her author dossiers one last time.

After walking into the cabin her nerves kicked in. She was going to see Sanford for the first time in months. Plus, this would be the first time they'd both be unattached at the same time. For a second, she felt a slight flicker of doubt, but she forced it back. She had come way too far to turn back now, and besides, he needed her. There was no way he knew any of these independent "indie" writers, and she would need to be the one to introduce him to them. The excitement began to overpower her nervousness, and she couldn't wait for the mixer to start.

"Hello, John," Sandy said as he and Micah exited their suite. John Cunningham was coming out of a cabin across from theirs.

"Sandy Morgan! I'm surprised you recognized me."

"Hah! You shouldn't be. I've been a reader and fan of your Buck Reilly series since you launched that first book. And this is my niece..."

"Micah. Nice to finally meet you in person." He turned back to Sandy, "We've been friends for a while through the TA social media writer's page. She's been quite an asset to the group, not just with her books, but donating time to help organize this cruise. Not to mention, getting you involved. I understand we sold out of cabins after you signed on, so that means a lot more readers will be exposed to the rest of us and our work as well. Thanks to both of you for that."

"I hope it will. Quite a list of some great writers aboard. Are you thirsty? We were heading over to see if we can't get the bar to open a tad early."

"The sun's way over the yardarm, so by all means, let's go. After you two." Cunningham held his arm out for the two of them to go on through the bulkhead door. They spied the Chesapeake Lounge across the atrium. Micah was happy that it was situated in the middle of the ship, where they'd be safer from the storm. The doors to the lounge were still closed when the trio arrived, but Sandy found they weren't locked and ushered them in.

"We don't open for another half hour," a bar server had approached them, looking like he wanted them to leave, but then Jason came in behind them. He'd seen Sandy and friends headed out early and figured this was where they were going.

"It's all right, Mr. Morgan and his friends are special guests of the captain. Please make them feel at home."

"Of course. What may I get for you?" The man had gone from openly irritated to smiling and accommodating as soon as Jason had appeared. By the time the other writers started wandering in, John and Micah were on their second rums, and Sandy was in rare form on his third Red Stripe.

The first two writers through the door were Kirk Jockell and Nick Sullivan. Both made a beeline for Sandy's table, though it was John and Micah they had recognized first. Halfway across the room, they realized who Sandy was, but they never broke their strides. Both men were extremely outgoing, and neither had ever met a stranger in their lives. Sandy took an instant liking to each of them and insisted they sit down. A couple of minutes later Nicholas Harvey walked over and introduced himself, his British accent catching Sandy by surprise.

Nick Sullivan said, "To keep things straight, we call him BritNick, and they call me HickNick, because of my Tennessee roots. We're both SCUBA fanatics, and we each have series with diving themes."

Sandy took another long, deliberate swig of his beer. "Bubble blowers, eh? Well, I guess that could work in a story, though I could never get beyond snorkeling and free diving when I lived back in the Keys. That was all I needed to bag a grouper or a few lobsters for supper. There's just something about the idea of having dozens of feet of water above my head, and that whole 'bends' thing that I couldn't get past. Never had to worry about that wearing just a mask and fins."

"It's a whole 'nother world, mate," BritNick said. "You get down on a reef sixty or seventy feet below, the colors having all gone dark. You use a flashlight looking under ledges and everything comes out in its true, ultrabright colors, it's fantastic! Nothing else like it. And then seeing all the creatures that only come out after dark when you do a night dive..."

"STOP! Sorry, Nick, but I have a huge phobia about being in any water outside of a bathtub or a pool after dark. You were about to give me nightmares," Sandy said.

John chuckled, "I'd have never figured you for that, Sandy."

"Hey, everybody has their private fears, John. Only a few of us admit 'em though. Another one of mine is running out of beer. HEY BARKEEP! How about another bottle," he yelled.

Micah winced at her uncle's loud voice, as several of the other writers turned and stared from around the room. She put a hand on Sandy's arm, "Sandy, don't you think you should pace yourself? The readers will start coming in any moment now."

"Don't be a killjoy, Micah. You know how I hate these things, and how much I've been dreading this one. But you know what, thanks to my new pals here, it might not turn out to be so bad."

Sandy's four male companions raised their glasses in support while Micah sighed. More writers were now headed toward their table, and Sandy directed them to drag chairs over. By the time the doors were opened to all the readers, most of the writers were well acquainted with each other, making it a less awkward, much more friendly mingling environment. Then it was time to stand up and greet all the incoming readers. Sandy was smiling, and Micah had never seen him smile at one of these "meet-and-greets" before. She'd arranged for the ship's photographer to be here, and he was getting some great shots that Sandy's publisher was going to be sure to love.

Another sudden attack of nerves had kept Donna confined to the head in her cabin, making her a half hour late to the meet-and-greet. By then it was a mob scene, with over three hundred people packed into what was the smallest lounge aboard the ship. The cruise director had picked it for the event because of its size, wanting a more intimate atmosphere, but had underestimated how many would attend.

She finally saw Sanford, but he was hemmed in by fans and a few of the other writers... and that damned Micah Monroe was cozied up next to him like they were already so familiar with each other. Too familiar. But right now, Donna couldn't see a way of getting over to Sanford without drawing a lot of attention to herself. She wanted Sanford's attention, but not everyone else's until after she had a chance to talk to him in private. With only one chance to make a first impression when they get reacquainted, Donna was going to have to pick the perfect opportunity, one when he was alone.

She saw that he was already mingling with several other authors and that Monroe chick was laughing and touching his arm like they were out on a date. That self-promoting, pretentious little bitch! Donna decided that she was going to have to do something about her.

"Ladies and gentlemen, if you'll excuse me for a minute, I'll be right back. The thing about beer is you can never buy it, you only rent it," Sandy said as he started weaving his way through the crowd in the direction of the "head."

Donna had perched on a stool at the far end of the bar where she could easily see Sanford. Half an hour into the mixer she saw him peel away from the group he'd been talking with. Sensing this was the perfect opportunity, she hopped off her stool and made her way a little less than gently through the crowd, garnering some irritated looks. She saw him enter a short corridor beyond the bar. When she got there, she realized it led to the restrooms. The women's was at the end on the left, and the men's right across from it. Knowing this might be her best chance to talk to him alone, she barged straight into the men's room. Ahead on the left behind a partition Sanford was relieving himself at a urinal.

"Hello, Sanford. You're a tough person to catch up to." Damn it, she thought, that was a lousy opening line.

"Whaaa? Hey lady, I think you made a wrong turn, this is the men's room. You need to get out of here."

"I know, but it's the only time I could catch you alone. You remember me, Donna?" She saw him glance at her, and there was no doubt about the look he gave her, it was recognition... mixed with concern. Not as welcoming as she had expected.

"Who says he's alone? And as he said, you need to get out of here." The voice came from behind the closed door of the toilet stall.

This wasn't how she'd planned it at all, Sanford was supposed to be alone in here. "And I need to have a private conversation with him. Would you mind leaving?"

The voice from the stall replied, "Are you serious? Yes, I would! Now you leave, or I'll come out there and make you leave, and that's *really* not something you want me to do right now."

Donna was flustered, she needed her conversation with Sanford to be just between the two of them. She considered waiting until the man in the stall left, but then Sanford said, "Lady, I'm not going to ask you again, get the hell out of here!"

She was shocked and confused that he was angry with her. It must be because that other man was within earshot; he couldn't seriously be mad. In a low voice, she said, "I'll wait for you outside."

"Don't wait for me anywhere! Get out of here, now!"

She retreated to the outside corridor, very confused about how Sanford had treated her. He had recognized her, that much she was certain of. Maybe she had overstepped her bounds by going into the men's room, especially with someone else in there. She'd apologize and explain after Sanford came out.

Sandy texted Micah, *"That Stage 5 Clinger is HERE, ambushed me in the head! May be waiting for me outside."*

Micah texted back, *"I'll handle it. Stay in there until I give you the all-clear"* He washed his hands and leaned back against the sink, waiting. Armand Rosamilia emerged from the stall, and Sandy said, "Thanks for the help," while automatically reaching his hand out.

Rosamilia replied, "You may want to wait a minute on that," and pointed to the sink.

"Oh. Right. Sorry." Sandy moved aside, giving Armand room. As he did, he heard a commotion outside the door.

"You get this a lot?" Armand asked.

"Not in here. I've had more than my share of drinks and beer bought for me, but this is a first, being stalked in a restroom by somebody. This is taking crazy to a whole new level."

Armand chuckled, "I hear you, that's completely out of bounds. We're here to talk with everybody but, there *are* limits."

"You'd think, right?"

There was a knock at the door and Micah's voice came through, "All clear!"

John and the two Nicks were waiting with her when Sandy and Armand emerged. "You guys dump her overboard?" Sandy asked when he didn't spot the Clinger.

"She saw the four of us coming, shot me a dirty look, then headed out. I don't know where she went, so you'll want to keep your eyes peeled. Since she went so far as to go into the men's room, I'm guessing she could pop up anywhere and she's not likely to give up that easily."

Sanford must've called that Micah person and her friends, who Donna recognized from their pictures in her research. It surprised her that he'd do that after she had made it clear she needed to talk to him in private. She'd now bide her time and catch him when he was alone, though now bathrooms were apparently off the list of the right places for that to happen. Since they chased her away from the bathroom area, she had gone back to the barstool where she could still see Sanford heading back to his spot. She'd waited this long to be with him, she could afford to be patient a little while longer.

Micah fingered her amulet and explained, "It was a Haitian mambo that gave us these; said she was repaying a 'life debt' to Sandy. They're supposed to protect us from harm. That chick was really wild-looking, and not in a good way."

John commented, "Sandy, it sounds like you're living out one of your books."

"On some days it seems like that, John. Though I've never cornered one of my characters in a bathroom by a crazy person before. I've got to remember and save this one."

The readers around him laughed, but the writers all knew he was serious. The best fiction has its roots in reality. Good writers know how to listen and observe people and events that happen around them, storing them as material to be used in future stories. Sandy was one of the best at this, finding more material in the marinas he visited than he could ever write about.

A lady in the crowd asked, "Since you use real-life events in your books to make them more realistic, then you must be upset about how Hollywood completely twisted and warped *Coastal Obsession*. The movie didn't come close to resembling the book, so much of it was either omitted or changed."

Sandy shook his head, "No, they aren't the ones who owed me the life debt." A few in the crowd chuckled. "Here's the deal; the check cashed, and that's what this is all about, it's a business. I try to write the best books that I can so people will read 'em and listen to the audiobooks. Those are the only places where I can guarantee you'll find them exactly the way I wanted them to be because I have the final say about them.

"To me, movies aren't about making 'great art.' Hollywood is interested in buying one of two things when they purchase the rights to books: a great story, or a big title that millions of people are already familiar with. In that first case, they'll reshape the story the way they think it should've been told, most often without regard to what the author intended. In the latter, they may get even farther off course from where the book was headed. Like with *Coastal Obsession*, which by the way will pay my bar tab for the next few years, as well as for this cruise." There was more laughter.

"But you know what? At that point they own it, so they can do whatever they want with it. You'll notice that the only place my name is credited in those movies is 'Based on the book by...' I don't demand creative control, and I don't want to get involved with making the damn things. I just want to write books. *You* are my audience, the people I aim to entertain, not those people who go to the movies or watch them on cable or satellite. Y'all are *my* people. We're all readers who would rather sit in our favorite chair and visualize what each character looks and sounds like, and that includes me. I love reading. We don't want it spoon-fed to us by a bunch of overpaid prima donna actors who can only regurgitate what the screenwriters put in front of them. There's something about having to use your brain and your imagination that makes reading a book so much more satisfying than watching a movie. No offense, HickNick." Sullivan was well-known in theater, movie, and television acting circles.

He laughed, "None taken. These days I do more writing and audiobook narration than acting anyway."

Sandy nodded then paused a minute to take a draw off his beer. "Don't get me wrong, if the movie is a hit, I'll be glad to take the credit as well as the cash, but if it's a stinker, at least my hands are clean."

There was more laughter over this. Sandy had connected with the entire crowd around him, all except for one person. That man stood on the edge of the group, wondering how such a beer-soaked has-been could garner the attention of so many people. These were sheep that obviously couldn't recognize top-tier writing when they saw it, versus the drivel from this big-name has-been.

After he and Micah had gone back to their suite to clean up for dinner, on the way out he told Jason, "Please send the captain our regrets, but we're going to eat with our readers. They paid a lot of money for this trip, and we're going to spend as much time with them as possible."

After they were out in the atrium Micah remarked, "Turning down the captain's dinner invitation to be with the readers. I'm impressed, Sandy."

"I got to thinking about how much I'd resent being snubbed at the very first dinner like that. I signed up to spend time with our readers, and that's exactly what I'm going to do. Besides, this is turning out to be a lot more enjoyable than I ever thought it would. Those writing pals of yours are a fun bunch and so are our readers. Maybe it's the comradery of the coastal genre folks, I don't know, but I'm enjoying myself."

"You should see what goes on in our chat room. It can get very much off the wall at times."

"Then I don't think I want to know about it."

Sandy picked a seat at a random table, much to the delight of the other diners. Less than half at that table were there because they were fans of his, but all were coastal fans. It was interesting to watch the interaction between his readers and those of some of the other writers, all advocating for their favorite books as well as their writers. He was able to pick up a lot of information about several of them.

Donna couldn't sit near Sandy since he filled the last seat at that table, and she ended up across the restaurant from him, which further irritated her. Several of her tablemates included David Berens and Jinx Schwartz who tried getting her to join in the conversation, but without any luck. Sitting silent and sullen, she ate quickly and left.

One thing Sandy learned at dinner was that Brian (B.R.) Spangler had five cats, something that blew his mind. After living several months with KC, he couldn't imagine having more cats than just him aboard. Then again, Spangler's house undoubtedly had much more square footage than his trawler.

Later he caught up with Spangler back at the Chesapeake Lounge. Most of the group who weren't interested in going to the casino or their cabins had ended up back there. That's when he learned that Brian also lived in Virginia, near the center of the state. Then they got back to their favorite common subject.

"It's not like they act as a pack, Sandy. Each has their favorite playing or 'hanging out' pals. Unless it's feeding time, you won't usually see them all together in one room," Spangler said.

"Unless KC is off 'hitting the head' somewhere or there's fish involved, he usually stays within sight of me." He told him the story of how he and KC met.

Spangler looked surprised. "You should feel honored. A bond that tight with a cat is a very rare thing. You know what they say, dogs have owners, but cats have staff. Sounds like you have found a real pal, instead."

John Cunningham joined them and heard the story too. "I have a cat named Stanley who watches while I write. He's a real character. I swear, sometimes when the story isn't coming to me, I can look at him and it's almost like he's silently communicating to me saying, 'I think Buck would do this.' And then it starts flowing again."

"Cats know things," Sandy commented.

Brian replied, "They do indeed."

Though the crowd in the lounge was smaller now, there were still enough people around that Donna didn't stand out from her barstool. She was getting angrier the more she watched. It was supposed to have been her job to introduce Sanford to all the other writers, but that damned Micah Monroe had beaten her to it. Since the bathroom incident, there hadn't been a time where he wasn't surrounded by people, often including Monroe. Like now.

Sanford didn't look like he was in a hurry to turn in tonight. As the crowd started shrinking, Donna became worried about being spotted and having another incident before they could have that private talk and she could explain things. She quietly slipped out before being noticed. Better to let things settle down overnight and try to catch Sanford alone in the morning.

15 CHANGE IS GOOD

First thing in the morning he checked over his equipment and "supplies," making certain that everything was in order and ready to go. It was all hidden under the false top layer in a box of books, glued together on a piece of thin plywood so they would come out as one unit. Unsure of how busy they would be after they reached the island, he went ahead and assembled the device. Placing it in an empty zippered bag, he then covered it with several layers of books before securing it with a small brass padlock. Not enough for any real security, but enough to keep the prying eyes of the housekeeping staff away.

He looked over at what was left in the book box before replacing the false lid. The tool for his least popular but most important part of the plan remained in there, though that part couldn't be carried out until closer to time. Now he only had to get through today and tomorrow.

"How'd you sleep, Sandy?"

"Surprisingly good, Micah. We must've outraced that storm; I didn't feel any pitching or rolling at all on this top-heavy sucker. And it looks like a beautiful and calm day out there. I'm looking forward to today's schedule. Let's go grab some breakfast, then we can come back, pick up our books, and get set up for the book signing."

"Wow, you're looking forward to a book signing? That's a first."

"I've been having fun talking with your coastal pals. In fact, I think we may change the afternoon's setup. It's different having so many other writers around, instead of being the sole focus. This is why I may want that change, but we can talk about it later. Meanwhile, keep an eye out for that clinger as we leave."

Micah was the first to spot the clinger as they entered the restaurant. Fortunately, she was already seated halfway across the room, and they picked a table as far away from her as possible. They were soon joined by Axel Blackwell and Doug Brisotti, both were also live-aboards, though the two of them lived on opposing coasts. The four were having an in-depth conversation about boats when they were interrupted.

"I'm glad to see that you were able to compare notes with Axel and Doug, Sanford since they both live on their boats. Though you don't have that in common with them anymore since now you live at your *Bayside* estate." Donna had appeared at Sandy's side after a stealthy approach. She glared at Micah before turning back to Sandy, who surprised her by looking angry. She had thought for sure he'd have been over the whole bathroom incident by now.

"Look lady, my name is Sandy, I only use Sanford on the books; I hate being called by that name. Just what estate are you talking about? I don't even live at *Bayside*, and I told you last night in the bathroom to get away from me."

Taken aback once again by his tone as well as his words, she replied, "They told me you live there! And for the record, you never told me to get away from you, only to leave the bathroom and not wait outside for you."

"Whoever told you I still live at *Bayside* doesn't know what they're talking about. Look, I've heard that you've been all over ESVA trying to find me, telling people we're close friends. I've never even met you before, and you need to learn to respect some boundaries. Here's the deal, I'll be happy to sign a book for you after we get all set up later, but until then please leave me alone."

Donna was almost as surprised as she was humiliated, and silently turned and walked out of the restaurant. Her humiliation quickly turned to anger after she left. Sanford or Sandy…whatever. Liar. He was nothing but a liar. They *did* know each other, he *recognized* her last night in the bathroom, she could see it on his face! But why would he want to deny knowing her in front of his friends? Was it because he was sitting with that Micah person?

Wait, did he say whoever told her that he *still* lived at *Bayside* was wrong? Meaning, he *had* lived there at one time. She *knew* it! She had to get him away from that Micah jerk, *she* must be why he was acting so strange. He *did* just ask her to come back and get a book signed; this must have been a covert message of some kind. Yes, of course! He was telling her to recreate the time they first met, back when there were others in the way of the two of them getting together. Only this time they'd get it right. Oh, and now she'd call him Sandy like all his other friends do.

Doug Brisotti remarked, "You were pretty restrained with that woman, I don't know if I could have been."

Sandy shrugged, "I think she's harmless. Annoying, but harmless. Just lives in her own little world, which unfortunately included the men's room last night." He went on to tell Doug and Axel the whole story about her trying to find out where he lived.

"Doug's right, that's really restrained. And yet you aren't worried," Axel said.

"Not really. As I said, she's delusional, but after thinking it over, I don't believe she's violent."

Micah stated, "Maybe you don't, but I don't trust her as far as I can throw her."

Axel said, "That's probably a good thing."

The ship had a large meeting room that had been set up with tables around the perimeter for the book signing portion of the schedule. A central cashier had been installed to handle selling all the books. Micah was sitting next to Sandy and was happy to see him enjoying himself, signing books, and taking pictures with readers. Many of those in line were also carrying copies of other participating authors' books. It looked like the whole cross-promotion idea was working.

Looking back through Sandy's line, she spotted the clinger, who seemed to be minding her manners for once. As Micah was busy with her readers, if there was going to be trouble it would take her a few seconds to get to Sandy, which worried her. A few minutes later the woman got up to the table.

"Hello, Sandy."

"Hello again." She handed him her copy as he asked, "Who do I make this out to?"

"Oh, that's right, we haven't been formally introduced yet, even though you know who I am. Donna. 'To my dear friend Donna.' I was hoping we could get together over lunch and talk."

He signed the book and handed it to her. "I'm sorry, I am trying to spend time with as many people as I can, so I need to sit with some other people that I haven't chatted with yet."

"But I'm your dear friend, Sandy. We need to spend time together. I have so much I need to say to you."

"Maybe later, Donna. But as you can see by all the folks behind you, I have a lot of books that need signing right now."

The woman behind her said, "Yeah, sweetie, you're burning up my time with Sandy. Move it along."

Donna spun around and faced her, "And I'm having a conversation with my close friend. A *private* conversation, so you need to bug off!"

Sandy said gently, "Donna, listen to me. You need to go now. You're keeping me from doing my job."

"Okay, Sandy, but we'll talk later, right?"

"Maybe later. But goodbye now."

Reluctantly, Donna turned and left, ignoring the strange looks she was getting from those in line who had overheard their conversation.

The woman who had been behind her moved up and handed her book to Sandy. "I saw what happened with her last night in the lounge. Watch yourself, Sandy, that chick is nuts."

At least now she'd gotten Sandy to put a name with her face. Of course, he'd known who she was before that, having recognized her from before the cruise. And while it hadn't gone exactly as she would've wanted since he was so busy right now, it was a good first step, all things considered. And they would be having a long talk next, she would make sure of that. After all, Sandy already agreed to meet her later. And after she told him everything she'd had to do to get free to be with him, he would probably have her move over to his cabin right away. She could hardly wait.

There was no sign of Donna during lunch, and she was quickly out of Sandy's mind as he enjoyed eating with a large table of readers as well as Chris Niles and Chip Bell. Micah was at the next table over, sitting with Douglas Pratt, but she was distracted, keeping an eye out for Donna. It wasn't the most fun lunch she'd had, not because of the company but because of who she had to watch out for.

During lunch, the crew had reconfigured the meeting room into more of a lecture hall with a podium and several hundred seats in front of it. Sandy grabbed the podium and wrestled it over to the side. Then with Micah's help, he placed twenty-one seats facing the audience. As people started streaming in, he guided the other authors up to the front.

"I know this was supposed to be a lecture by me this afternoon, but I can't think of anything more boring than to hear me talk about myself. Over the past twenty hours, I've enjoyed getting to know many of these folks that you see up here, and I think you will too. That's why we're all going to have an open discussion on anything that y'all want to ask us or talk about.

"I've read books by several of these folks, and when I get back home, I'm going to work my way down the rest of the list. I urge you to do the same and leave reviews for the ones you like. But in the meantime, do yourself a favor and get to know them all. So, let's start by taking the first question..."

"Nice move, having everyone else join in, Sandy." Evan Graver had wheeled up in his chair. "This thing has taken on more of an extended family reunion feel to it than a book cruise. I've sold and signed a lot more books than I thought I would."

Sandy raised his ever-present beer in a salute. "Thanks for jumping in. I was dreading that last bit, but it turned out to be a lot of fun for everybody. Beats listening to me drone on about myself and my books for over an hour."

He was furious. Not only had he been stuck on the end seat away from the central focus, no one had directed a single question specifically to him. Then when he tried to join in the discussion, people talked over him, both the other authors as well as the audience. Now standing by the lounge entrance, he was getting only polite nods as people passed by. To top it all off, he hadn't sold a quarter of the books he'd brought along, and his signing line had been the shortest one.

That's okay, he thought. After tomorrow he'd sell a lot of books, especially the new one that he'd yet to write. The one about being the sole surviving author of the cruise. He smiled, then left to go to the ship's casino. He knew his luck was about to change.

16 A STICKY SITUATION

The next morning Sandy was up and dressed early, out on his balcony watching as they pulled into Bermuda. The pilot boat came out to meet the ship, then they slowly made their way into the cruise ship berths. Situated on a large manmade jetty called the North Arm, just inside what would be the point on a hook-shaped part of the island. Or rather, one of the islands. Contrary to popular belief, Bermuda isn't a single landmass. It's a combination of over a hundred islands and islets, the larger ones linked by bridges and roads. Being out on this point of land allows the deep draft cruise ships the depth they need, while still affording the protection of the peninsula.

The crew threw the heaving lines to dockworkers on shore who pulled the heavier mooring lines over to the bollards. Winches on the ship pulled the lines tight, and then the gangways were lowered.

"Penny for your thoughts," Micah said as she joined Sandy and handed him a coffee.

"I'm thinking a water taxi to breakfast in Hamilton, then a tour of the Goslings rum factory, some shopping, lunch with drinks—preferably Dark-n-Stormies—then maybe more shopping or more drinks, depending on how good the bartender is."

"Nice plan. Fill out this customs card Jason gave me, then we can get going."

He removed the false top in the box again. The tools for the second part of the plan were just where he'd left them. He dreaded the idea of using them and decided to put that out of his mind temporarily. After this was over, it will have all been worth it.

Donna dressed quickly and went to the restaurant nearest to the VIP cabins where she'd seen Sandy going. Taking her time and eating slowly she kept her eyes open to spot him. Now that they'd developed a rapport, she was sure today he'd be wanting to spend the day with her. But after a leisurely breakfast and three cups of coffee, there'd been no sign of him. Maybe he wasn't a breakfast person after all.

She decided to check out the VIP cabin area, maybe she could run into him over there. The man at the desk just inside the double doors asked if he could help her.

"I'm looking for my friend, Sandy Morgan."

Not knowing the recent history between Donna and Sandy, Jason said, "Mr. Morgan and Miss Monroe left quite a while ago."

Donna bristled at the idea that once again Micah Monroe was apparently with Sandy, but she kept her composure. "I didn't see him at the restaurant across the hall."

"I believe they've gone to town for the day. Would you care to leave either of them a message?"

"No, I'll catch up to him later." This guy just didn't get that she was Sandy's friend, not Micah's.

"I'm afraid he has a rather busy day ahead. Are you certain you wouldn't like to leave a note?"

"I think I'll catch up to him at dinner when he comes back."

"I'm afraid he won't be dining aboard ship; the authors are all taking a boat to a dinner with the governor this evening. But tomorrow he is scheduled to be back in the meeting room for most of the day, you can certainly find him then."

"Thank you."

Donna reasoned that If he was going to have dinner with the governor, he would be coming back to clean up here first. Suddenly she had an idea. The governor was going to be minus one dinner guest. There had to be a lot of gift shops and a hardware store in Hamilton, so she could find everything she needed there.

"Great Dark-n-Stormies!" Sandy said.

"I take it my shopping run is over?" Micha sounded disappointed.

"Not at all. Keep piling it all up here, and I'll keep an eye on it, along with my rum." He'd done some damage at Goslings Rum Company.

"Take it easy on those Stormies, Sandy. We've got an important dinner to go to."

"There's not a politician in the world who could stand between me and my drinks, at least none with any sense." He smiled and winked at her. "Relax, I'll pace myself. You do the same at those shops."

"I'll do my best. See you in a bit."

He leaned back and texted Betsy, telling her how much he was enjoying Bermuda and meeting all the other writers and readers. Though he said he wasn't looking forward to the governor's dinner tonight. Politics and politicians were way down on his list of things he enjoyed.

A few hours later Donna returned to the VIP section, addressing the man at the desk, "I decided to take you up on your idea of leaving a note, but I also wanted to leave this rum cake along with it. Would you please see that it gets put in his room right away... Jason?" She smiled when she spotted his name tag, and she placed a box with the cake along with an envelope on his desk.

"I will see to it myself. Bermudan rum cakes are such a thoughtful and iconic gift, I'm sure he will enjoy it."

Like he would know what Sandy likes or doesn't like, she thought. She hesitated until Jason stood, picked up the box, and started across the lobby area. She turned as if to go back out but was moving slowly enough to see with an over-the-shoulder glance that he had gone through the last door on the left. The cabin was down next to the aft sitting area. Now she went over to the Chesapeake Lounge, picking a seat that had a clear view of the VIP cabin area entrance. All she had to do was wait, and hope that Sandy didn't come back too early.

The water taxi took Sandy and Micah back to the landing next to the ship. They got one of the crew members to help bring all their purchases aboard using a hand truck. Running behind schedule, they hurried up to their cabin. They had half an hour to get cleaned up before they had to meet another chartered water taxi. This boat would shuttle them across the five-mile stretch of open water to Flatts Village, one of the oldest settlements in Bermuda. It was here at a waterfront estate that the dinner would be held. By taking a direct route from North Arm, the boat ride would take a fraction of the time a van would need to go all the way around the "hook" on the island's curving, narrow roads.

Donna searched her brain for an idea as to how she could get that guy away from his desk so she could carry out the next part of her plan without being seen. Fortunately, providence smiled down on her as she saw Jason come out through the door and head around the atrium with a magazine under his arm. He ducked through a door marked "Staff Only," and she hoped he'd be in there awhile.

Getting up, she grabbed her bag from the hardware store. Casually glancing around, she made her way through the VIP doors and down to Sandy's cabin door. Rather than knock, she took out a large double plunger of quick-setting, ultra-strength epoxy from the bag. It had a built-in mixing nozzle with a pointed applicator, perfect for what she needed to do. She quickly applied the epoxy all around between the door and the doorframe, filling the gap between them.

Now all she needed was for this to have about five minutes to set, and Sandy wouldn't be making that boat to meet the governor. Instead, he'd have a hole in his schedule for dinner. Once the maintenance crew extricates him from that cabin, she'll "accidentally" run into him in the atrium and suggest they have dinner together. Meanwhile, she went back to the lounge to wait. A minute after she sat down, Jason returned from his bathroom run. Donna smiled as she thought, timing is everything.

"What the hell?" Sandy tried going out their door, only to find it jammed.

"Let me try, Sandy." Micah pulled the handle with all her might, but with no results.

Sandy pushed a button on the cabin's phone.

"Concierge, how may I help you?"

"Jason, it's Sandy. Our door's jammed, and we can't get out! Come push it while I pull."

"I will be right there, Sandy."

Jason saw the handle move, and he pushed the door hard. Nothing. Again, he saw the door handle move, and he launched himself at the middle of the door. All he succeeded in doing was bruising his shoulder. He heard Sandy yelling from inside. He yelled back, "I'll get help from Engineering."

John Cunningham walked out of his room and gave him a quizzical look. "What's all the yelling about?"

"Mr. Morgan's door is jammed, and they can't get out. I'm going to get Engineering to help."

John went over to Sandy's door and was about to try pushing on it when he spotted the bead of epoxy that ringed it. He walked over to Jason who was on the phone and said, "Better tell them to bring a small reciprocating saw. Somebody glued their door shut."

"What! Are you certain about that?"

"Jason, I've seen and smelled enough quick hardening epoxy to recognize it. There are only two ways of getting that loose; heat it with a torch, which I don't recommend, or use a thin saw blade. It'll take a while to do either. In any case, I don't think he's going to make our boat."

After hearing what happened from Jason, Sandy sighed and grabbed a beer out of the bar fridge. He went out on the balcony and sat down. A few minutes later a dejected Micah joined him.

"There's no way they'll get us out in time to catch the boat," she said.

"Kind of figured that. Sorry, kiddo."

"Sorry for me, you mean. You didn't want to go."

Sandy took a swig of his beer and then said, "I wasn't looking forward to the political aspect of it. I get that it's going to be a great plug for their tourism board, but we both know the governor will use it for his own purposes. I'm no fan of politicians."

"What about Candi, Eric's girlfriend? She's an ex-member of Congress. You like her, don't you?"

"Candi's different. She got in to make a difference. She got out when she saw more than her share of corruption and had enough of the crap that came with the job. I admire her for that."

"Maybe this governor is like her."

"Don't care. Not my country, not my politics. Want a beer? I'm getting another."

She sighed. "Sure, since we're going nowhere fast."

~

The tourist board photographer asked, "Where's Sandy Morgan?" She wanted to get a shot of all the authors together on the wharf before they boarded the boat.

John Cunningham said, "Someone glued his door shut. No way he's making the boat or the dinner."

Presley Peterson asked, "Who would do something like that?"

John replied, "He's got that crazy woman hounding him, she'd be high on my suspect list."

"Whatever, we'll just have to do this without him. Okay, form a line on either side of Mr. Graver," the photographer said as she arranged all twenty of them. As she took her shot, one of the other passengers on the North Arm also took a photo with their phone. Then the writers all boarded the water taxi for the twenty-minute trip, a fraction of what it would've taken by car.

"Cunningham and Graver are both fishermen. I'm thinking of inviting them up for a few days of fishing after I get a new center console rig," Sandy said. "This has been the best part of the trip so far, meeting other folks who love writing and the water as much as I do."

"As we do," Micah corrected him. "But yes, that's partly why I'm glad I got involved with this group. Good folks."

"Good folks that left without us. There they go," Sandy pointed to the water taxi as it made its way past the ship, about sixty feet below their balcony.

"Can't blame them. It wasn't like we were going to rappel down from this balcony." Micah looked disappointed.

"Tell you what, I'll buy you the very best meal available aboard ship tonight."

She chuckled. "You know that with the VIP cabins, everything is included, right? So, you've already bought me that dinner."

"If I had known that I'd have been scarfing up caviar for breakfast. And I don't even like caviar!"

Micah laughed, "I heard that lobster goes great with eggs."

"Yes, and beer goes great with sitting out on the balcony. Get yourself a fresh one while you bring me one, too."

Micah frowned at him, "Lazy."

"Relaxing. Recovering from paying the tab for all this." He smiled back at her.

Micah checked on the door where workmen were still using a reciprocating saw to free them. Grabbing two beers from the refrigerator and returning to the balcony, she handed one to Sandy before sitting down herself.

"Where are they?" she asked him.

Sandy pointed off in the distance at the boat. It was mostly a dot now; they could no longer see the people on board. As they watched, the dot became engulfed by a huge orange fireball, followed by a mushrooming plume of smoke mixed with fire. A little over five seconds later the sound of an explosion reached them. The boat was gone, as were probably all its occupants. The two of them could do nothing more than stare in stunned silence.

17 UNANSWERED QUESTIONS

Jason stepped out onto the balcony, "We've managed to free the door, but I'm afraid you've missed the boat." He noticed the strange looks on both their faces and turned to see what they were looking at. "Oh, no! That looks bad."

"That," Sandy said, "was the boat we were supposed to have been on. We've got to get out there and help search for our friends."

"There may be some boats at the water taxi docks. Though it looks like help may already be on the way."

They could see several boats racing out from the harbor in the direction of the explosion. Sandy said, "Let's go."

The two of them hurried out of the ship and then down the North Arm to the ferry docks. A large crowd was already gathering there at the now empty dock. A bald man with a long white beard and a gold hoop earring had retreated inside a small ticket booth, a tear running down his face. A sign attached to the booth proclaimed this to be the home of Winsten's Water Taxi Service. Sandy started to approach the window to ask if he knew where there was a boat he could rent but was intercepted by a young man.

"Best to leave Stenny be right now, mister."

"I wanted to see if I could rent a boat and go help search for... wait, did you say 'Stenny'?"

"Yeah, his real name's Arthur Winsten, but everybody around the docks here calls him Stenny. That was one of his boats that just blew up. Besides, every boat around here that's running already took off to go help."

The VHF radio in the ticket booth announced, "I've got a survivor on board! Heading for the dock at Hamilton, have an ambo meet me there to take him to King Edward Memorial, he's got burns." Another voice came across the speaker, "Hamilton harbormaster here, roger that, we'll have EMS standin' by."

"Tell all the other boats to take their time, this guy was the only one who made it."

Micah stared at Sandy in shock as she realized she had watched almost two dozen of her friends and acquaintances die a few minutes ago.

"We need to get to that hospital to help identify the survivor. Maybe notify his family," she said.

Sandy nodded somberly, "Let's get a taxi."

On the ride over to the hospital, Micah said, "Did you hear what the name of the water taxi owner was? Stenny. That was the Stenny boat, Sandy."

"It's just a coincidence, Micah. A funny coincidence."

She fingered her amulet. "Another one. Right after we get locked in our cabin so we can't make the boat, then it blows up. Like someone knew ahead of time that the boat was going to explode. As in rigged it to blow up but made sure we weren't on board."

"So, you think this was all orchestrated by some voodoo witch from Miami?" He sounded disgusted.

"She's a mambo, not a witch. And for the record, I don't think she orchestrated it, but I think she foresaw something or knew something, not necessarily made something happen."

"I think we were locked in by that whack job reader who won't leave me alone. I think she wanted us, or me, to miss that boat. Did she cause it to blow up? I have no idea. Did she know it was going to explode? Again, I don't know."

The cabbie was quiet, listening to every word. Like everyone else on the island, he'd already heard about the explosion. After overhearing their conversation, he was now very uneasy. He couldn't wait to discharge this fare and then go find the nearest constable. Somebody needed to check out these two's stories.

Betsy was having drinks and dinner with Mimi at the *Cove Beach Bar* when she happened to glance up at the flat screen over the bar. Usually, it showed the latest fishing videos taken from boats in the marina or a live sport of some kind. But today someone had switched it over to a news channel instead. The volume was muted, but the closed captioning was running on the bottom of the screen. The video was of open water with a lot of flame and smoke, obviously taken by a smartphone at a long distance. She read the captioning: *"... the group of several dozen authors were on a chartered boat, headed for a private dinner with the governor of Bermuda. Unconfirmed reports say that Sanford Morgan, the New York News bestselling author was part of the group and may have been on board when the explosion occurred. A sole survivor has been taken to King Edward VII Memorial Hospital, though his or her identity and condition aren't yet known."*

Mimi saw Betsy's face go pale. "What is it, Bets?"

Betsy pointed at the screen, her finger shaking, "Sandy texted me that he was taking a boat to dinner with the governor tonight. That was the boat." She choked up.

"It's youse gals' lucky night, ya each get to buy me a beer." Baloney had spotted the two of them and figured they would be good for a round or two. As he walked up, he saw the shocked look on both their faces. "What's the matter?"

Mimi replied, "Sandy was on that boat."

Bill's eyes swung to the screen and his face fell. He took the unlit cigar out of his mouth and stuck it in his pocket, all thoughts of beer now the furthest thing from his mind as he plopped down into an empty chair. "He can't a been on that boat. He can't be..." Baloney didn't finish the sentence; he didn't have to. All three were thinking the same thing, and silently praying for it not to be true.

Mimi texted Casey, telling him to turn on the cable news. A minute later he called her, "Do we know any more than this?"

"No, nothing. Betsy, Baloney, and I are watching it at the *Beach Bar*."

"Y'all come over to the *Lady Dawn*, I'll call Eric. He's got a house over there and knows a lot of people. If anyone can find out anything from stateside, he can."

On the way over to Casey and Dawn's boat, Betsy tried calling and texting Sandy. The calls went straight to voicemail, and the texts showed they were never read.

Jeff was sitting with Casey and Dawn in the salon, looking completely distraught. After Casey called him, he'd tried Micah's number, with the same results as Betsy. Casey was just hanging up with Eric.

"He's going to call me back after he makes some calls."

Lindsay and Murph came in, Lindsay going straight over to sit with Jeff and Dawn, those three being Micah's closest friends. None were accepting of the idea that Micah and Sandy had been on that boat and were now gone. They all were holding out hope for a miracle.

Micah and Sandy arrived at the hospital at the same time as the ambulance. As the rear doors opened and the gurney was removed, they recognized Presley Peterson. He was wearing a short sleeve shirt and Bermuda shorts, and the unprotected parts of his legs and arms were burned. Still, he looked much better than they would've expected, having been through that blast. He looked over and recognized them as he was being wheeled inside.

"Why weren't you two on the boat with all of us? What did you know that we didn't? Why didn't you tell us? Did you have something to do with this? They're dead, all of them!" The doors of the Emergency Room closed behind the gurney.

A reporter had been filming the exchange, and now a constable came over and led them next to a police car where he began asking questions. Two minutes later another constable approached them with the taxi driver who said, "That's them, they're the ones! I picked them up at the ferry docks."

The constable conferred with the one who had been questioning them then led Sandy and Micah to separate police cars, which quickly sped away.

As the group watched the TV and waited for a call from Eric, the announcer said, "We have breaking news about that boat explosion on Bermuda. Bestselling author Sanford Morgan was not aboard the boat, but he and a female companion were just taken into custody for questioning. The Bermuda police are now investigating this as a criminal act instead of an accident. Here is a new video we've just received of Morgan being detained." The footage from the hospital included Peterson being wheeled in on the gurney while yelling at Sandy and Micah. Then it showed the two of them being loaded into the back of the police cars and driven off. "The Chief Constable of Bermuda is expected to make a statement within the hour, and we'll bring that to you as it happens."

Two minutes later, Casey's phone rang. He put it on speaker, "Hey Eric, I've got the gang here with me. I guess you just saw that latest video, and that at least Sandy and Micah are alive and safe."

"Alive, maybe, but I wouldn't say safe. I've sent my Bermuda lawyer to represent the two of them, to protect their rights. Since this has now gone out to the international media, the authorities are going to be in a big hurry to get to the bottom of it. Pinning it on foreigners will be better for them than Bermudans. I'm flying over there now. If any of you want to come along, I can pick you up at the Norfolk International private terminal in forty-five minutes. You'll need to bring a passport and a change of clothes. We don't know what we'll be getting into over there."

In a somber Bermudan accent, the Chief Constable said, "Twenty-one persons lost their lives in the explosion, including the captain and mate, who were Bermudans. The other nineteen were part of a group of American authors from a visiting cruise ship and were en route to a private dinner with the governor. None of these names will be released until their relatives are properly notified. There was, however, one survivor, Mr. Presley Peterson, who remains in hospital with second-degree burns on his arms and legs but is expected to be released perhaps as soon as tomorrow.

"Our investigators have already determined that this was no accident. The boat was diesel-powered, and diesel is not prone to exploding. It takes both compression and heat for that to happen, so we suspect some sort of explosive device was planted near the fuel tank. By whom and to what purpose is what we are now trying to ascertain.

"We have detained three American citizens for questioning, Mr. Sanford Morgan, Miss Micah Monroe, and Ms. Donna DuBois. We have not charged any of them with a crime at present, though under Bermuda law we can detain them for up to twenty-four hours before doing so."

Fifteen hundred miles away Deputy Linton leaned forward in his easy chair at home, not believing what he had just heard. A Donna DuBois was being questioned in another apparent multiple homicide. Could it be their Donna DuBois? If it was, at least they knew where she was, for now. Though a lot of good it did them since there were no funds available for him to fly to Bermuda to question her if this was the right Donna. Plus, he didn't even own a passport.

He was able to find the number for the Hamilton authorities online and called to tell them what he suspected. They needed to know there was more of a pattern developing with Donna DuBois if this was indeed the same woman.

❧

The attorney walked into the interrogation room and said, "I need to speak to my client in private."

Sandy looked surprised, but the investigator looked irritated. He got up slowly, glaring at the attorney as he did, but he left the two alone.

"Who the hell are you," Sandy asked.

"Lucien Armitage, your solicitor." He held out his hand to shake, which Sandy reluctantly did.

"You've got the right name for the job, but I didn't ask for you or any other attorney."

"True. But your friend, Eric Clarke, sent my associate and me to represent both you and Ms. Monroe. My associate is with her now. Mr. Clarke will be arriving within the next couple of hours, by the way."

Sandy was surprised. "How did Eric know..."

"You have made the international news, Mr. Morgan. Mr. Clarke has a residence here in Bermuda, and I handle his affairs on the island. He has a lot of friends here, including the governor. But friendships only go so far, and I'm going to need to know everything you do if you're to make any friends with the Bermuda constables."

"It's Sandy. Call me Sandy. International news? Oh boy, I'm going to be in deep crap with my publisher over this."

Lucien laughed, "Not if I have anything to say about it. Now, let's start at the beginning. Tell me exactly what transpired."

Lucien and his associate turned out to be excellent attorneys. Under their watchful eyes, Sandy and Micah told their stories, from the ESVA stalker to the mambo, the Stenny boat, and their epoxied door which was also verified by Jason. He had been brought in briefly for questioning before being allowed to return to his ship.

The police even viewed the voodoo parts of their story as potentially credible. Though not one of the most mainstream beliefs of the island nation, due to the historical influences from the Caribbean and Africa on their island's culture, voodoo was accepted locally as a legitimate religion. For this reason, that part of their combined story was viewed as also being truthful.

A little after two a.m. the two of them were released; their phones and passports that had been confiscated at the beginning of the interrogations were returned at that point. Then they were stunned to see Casey, Dawn, Betsy, Jeff, and Baloney waiting for them in the hallway along with Eric.

"Sheesh, the things I gotta go through to get you to buy me a beer, you hack," Baloney said.

A tired and disheveled Sandy smiled at him, "Your turn to buy, I'm fresh out." He turned and hugged Betsy, saying, "I know you said you loved this place, but I can't wait to go home."

She grinned ruefully at him and said, "I can't wait to get you home, either."

"We figured you might need a ride since your other one sailed a couple of hours ago," Eric said.

"I appreciate that, Eric. And for you arranging for Lucien, too. We might still be in those interrogation rooms or worse if he hadn't shown up."

"No problem, Sandy. Let's get out of here while the getting is still good. You need to be ready because there's a throng of reporters outside looking for updates on this story and especially your part in it."

Eric hadn't overstated it, as numerous microphones were stuck in Sandy's face while cameras recorded them all leaving the police station and later boarding Eric's private jet.

On the slightly more than an hour-long trip back to Norfolk in Eric's Gulfstream 800, Baloney finally got his beer, and everyone got to hear Sandy and Micah's full story of what had happened. In return, they learned about the Chief Constable's statement. Their initial elation on heading home then slowly turned to sadness as they reflected on the lives of the people that had been lost.

Sandy said, "I'd just met them, but they all seemed nice, and a few felt like I'd known them for years. I hate to say it but the only one that I didn't take to was the guy who survived, Presley Peterson. It seemed like he was pointing the finger at Micah and me, all because we missed the boat."

Micah agreed, "He did. But he'd just been through an explosion, so it isn't fair to judge him on that. Yeah, those were some great people we lost. Very talented ones as well, some of the best in coastal and islands writing. Ironically, now their sales will undoubtedly increase because of the publicity, but they won't be here to enjoy it."

Baloney asked, "Won't yours too?"

She nodded slightly, "Probably. The old saying is that any publicity is good publicity, so long as they spell your name right. But this sure as heck isn't the way I wanted to build sales, off the deaths of my friends."

"I didn't mean..."

"I know, Bill. I'm sorry, it's just been a long day."

He nodded solemnly, then brightened. "Hey, let me buy you another one of Eric's beers."

That brought a smile as she reached over and patted his arm. "Deal."

18 UNFINISHED BUSINESS

"I'm telling you, I had nothing to do with what happened to that boat!" Donna had been placed in a cell by the investigator after having been taken out of the interrogation room. Now, many hours later, he was back to explain what was to happen to her.

"We believe you. We are no longer detaining you in connection with the explosion. But you are to be deported as an undesirable person and sent back to the States."

"But you know I had nothing to do with that!"

"With the boat incident, that's true. However, we could charge you with the unlawful false imprisonment of Sanford Morgan and his niece aboard that cruise ship in Bermudan territorial waters. Instead, we have decided to deport you, and ban you from re-entering our country in the future." He didn't add that she was going to have a 'greeting party' waiting at the US airport who wanted to talk to her about the now suspected homicides of her husband and son.

"What false imprisonment?"

"The one in which you used epoxy to glue his door shut. The hardware store clerk picked out your photo."

Donna was chagrinned, never considering the possibility of being caught while still in Bermuda. "Wait, did you say his *niece*?"

"Yes, his sister's daughter, Miss Monroe."

Despite her current circumstances, Donna was relieved. Sandy wasn't dating Micah; they were only traveling together. "How soon am I getting out of here?" She was anxious to get back to America and to find Sandy and apologize. Then to take him up on that lunch rain check he had given her. Or wait, had she given him one? It didn't matter, they'd have lunch.

"You are booked on tomorrow's morning flight to Charlotte, and then from there to Norfolk. You may claim your belongings at the cruise ship terminal the day after tomorrow when the ship docks. They will gather it all and have it waiting for you." And, he thought, you can say hello to your welcoming committee.

As he lay in his hospital bed in Bermuda, he knew it wasn't finished yet. They both had to disappear so his story was the only one that would be written. They weren't supposed to be alive. The cops told him that some nut job had glued their cabin door shut, which is why they missed the boat. Just his luck, they were saved by some stalker. Both were supposed to have been on that boat and like everyone else, blown to bits.

The looks of surprise on the faces of the ones that were aboard as he jumped off the back into the water were priceless. Pressing the detonator as he hit the surface and dove under, he hadn't expected the underwater concussion to be as bad as it was. He surfaced in time to see bits of the boat and body parts raining down, then he quickly pulled off his long sleeve shirt and long pants. He had sewn small lead weights in each, ensuring they would sink and not be found amongst the floating wreckage.

Another thing he hadn't fully anticipated was how much the salt water would sting his arms and legs. In the privacy of his cabin, he had used a propane torch to create burns mimicking what he thought he would have gotten had he been closer to the blast. It had hurt like hell, but it was the only way he could get away without suspicion falling on him.

After he hit the water, the pain was even more excruciating as the salt attacked the burns. He didn't have to act about being in agony as he was plucked from the water by the first boat on the scene. But the ends would justify the means. The sales of his first book would surely skyrocket, and he probably would get an agent and an advance for his story about the ill-fated cruise and boat explosion. He was going to be just as famous as Sandy Morgan, if not more so.

For the next few days, he had to act partially deaf and slightly disoriented, like he should be if he had been closer to the explosion. He could pull that off, easily enough. But now there was that unexpected complication of Morgan and his niece surviving. This presented two hurdles, the first being their deaths had to look like an accident. He could figure out how to accomplish that easily enough. But before that could happen, he'd need to find them. That was hurdle number two.

Presley was due to be discharged later today, and the cruise line had booked him into a hotel then on tomorrow morning's flight to Charlotte. After that, on to Norfolk where he'd collect the belongings he'd left aboard the ship. Then he'd start the hunt. So far, he'd managed to accomplish this much, how hard could it be to find Morgan?

Sandy woke up back on his boat, with one familiar weight on his side, and one not so familiar. Looking over, he saw that KC was perched just above a human arm that was slung across his side. The cat's eyes were boring into his.

"I'm guessing you want breakfast, and that you've forgiven me for being gone for a few days."

Betsy's voice came from behind his back, "Are you talking to me, or KC?"

"Yes."

She laughed, and her arm tightened around him. "In that case, yes also. What time is it?"

He looked at the clock beside the bunk, "Ten. We managed to get a whole five hours of sleep after we got back."

She replied, "Almost five, but it was worth losing those extra few minutes."

"Ouch!"

"I wasn't complaining, Sandy."

"Not that, KC just clawed me."

"Meaning that it's time to feed us both."

After feeding KC, the two went to the *Cove* deck for a late breakfast. Mimi greeted him with a big hug.

"We thought you were gone, Sandy."

"I never thought I'd be so happy to have an obsessive fan." He gave her a quick rundown about what happened.

"I'm sorry about your friends."

"Mostly acquaintances, but a few were well on their way to being friends, some I'd hoped would come here and fish with us. I feel terrible for their families and friends."

Mimi asked, "Do they have any idea who did this and why? And were you and Micah also targets?"

He sighed, "The last I heard they still hadn't figured that out. But if we were, there's no safer place for us to be than right here."

"True. Where we can all keep an eye on you."

Back aboard *Epilogue* after breakfast, Sandy and Betsy were sitting on the open aft deck.

"Well, I had better be going, and let you get back to work on your next book," Betsy said.

"No, you don't. This whole thing has gotten me thinking and feeling kind of mortal. These past few years I've enjoyed writing, connecting with my readers, and building a following and a career. I've made more money than I can spend, but it's only money after all. Maybe the time has come to make this boat earn its name in my life. I mean, what do I have left to prove? I wanted to give Micah some help to get her started, and I've done that. Her last book was great, it has great reviews and a high ranking. There's nothing left for me to teach her."

"If you don't write, what are you going to do?"

"Betsy, you know we're only given so many days on this Earth. I don't think I want to squander the ones I have left by sitting at a keyboard, staring at a screen every day. I want to spend time with my friends. And I'd love to spend a lot of it in the cockpit of a sportfisherman fishing with you, while I still can. Does that sound like something you'd be interested in?"

She studied his face, a worried look coming over her own. "I'm not interested in getting married again, Sandy."

"Good, because I'm not either, and that wasn't what I was asking. I like spending time with you partly because you're a damn good fisherman. A big part of that is how we enjoy talking with each other. I think authors are driven to write because they feel a need to communicate. I still do, just to a smaller audience."

She was quiet for a minute then said, "I guess in a way this is what I was looking for when I came up here. I only realized exactly how much I wanted it when I thought I saw you die on TV yesterday. So, yes, that sounds exactly like something I'd be interested in." As if he'd been listening to the conversation and wanted to give his stamp of approval, KC jumped up in her lap and lay down. "Looks like it's unanimous."

A few minutes later Micah arrived; it was obvious she had something on her mind. "Sandy, I need to talk to you."

Betsy asked, "Would you like me to go?"

"No, please stay, Betsy, this isn't that personal or earth-shattering. I just wanted to tell you that Jeff and I signed a lease on a place this morning. It's only a few minutes away, and if you need me, I can be over in a flash, but I think I want to focus on my writing now."

Sandy beamed, "That's great, kiddo! I'm happy for you guys. Don't worry about me and the boat anymore, I'm not planning any long trips, and I can always hire a kid off the docks to keep this tub washed and waxed. By the way, I have a bit of news myself, I've decided to retire."

Suddenly Micah had a "deer in the headlights" look and sat down heavily in a chair. "What do you mean, retire?"

"I mean, quit writing. I'm going to go fishing instead. And I'm dragging Betsy here along with me, kicking and screaming."

"I wouldn't exactly put it that way, Sandy," Betsy retorted.

"But what about your readers," Micah asked.

"We write along the same lines. I know you wanted to make it all on your own without anyone knowing we're related. Well, that cat is out of the bag after Bermuda, and now you have a lot of international exposure. I'm going to suggest to my readers that they try your books since I can do that now without giving away any family secrets."

"What about your publisher?"

"I've fulfilled my last contract with her, and besides, she's made plenty of money off me. I'll be very surprised if you don't hear from her yourself since you're definitely on her radar now."

"I don't want you to push me on her."

"Why would I do that? You've made your way up to this point, and I'm not going to start interfering now."

"Wow. I just never thought of you as the retiring type, Sandy."

"Active retirement. Fishing, hanging with my pals, buying a new outboard that I can use to run around the bay, that kind of retirement."

Betsy spoke up, "Why buy a new outboard when you can always use mine?"

"Because I have to get a couple of drinks in you before you'll let me run the damn thing!"

"Okay, maybe we can work on getting you more helm time," she grinned.

He rolled his eyes in reply.

Micah watched the playful interaction between the two, knowing there was much more to his decision than what happened in Bermuda. No doubt that played a big part in pushing it along, but it wasn't the only factor. It's funny how the biggest changes in both Sandy's and her lives were now happening simultaneously. She was happy for those two, as well as for herself and Jeff.

"Well, if it's okay with you, Jeff and I are going to go furniture shopping today."

Sandy replied, "Of course it is. You're going to go work for yourself now. But before you're totally off the payroll, could you do something for me tomorrow afternoon? How about picking up our things from the cruise terminal after that big barge gets back into port? Maybe you can combine it with a morning shopping trip too?"

"Not a problem." She stood up, "Hey, I'm happy for you, Sandy. You too, Betsy."

Betsy replied, "Same to you, Micah. Jeff as well."

After Micah left, Sandy said, "That went much better than I thought it would. I was anticipating having to push that bird out of the nest, but she learned to fly all on her own."

Betsy nodded, "Not just fly, soar; you won't need to worry about her. I read her latest book while you were gone, and she's good. After all this exposure, she'll do fine."

"Especially after I sic my publisher on her."

"I thought you said you weren't going to do that!"

"No, I asked her if she *thought* I'd do that. If she had, she'd have realized that of course, I would." He smiled. "But I'm not going to push; I'm only going to suggest that she take a long look at her. She's a very smart woman, she recognizes talent when she sees it. After all, she gave me a contract, didn't she?"

It was Betsy's turn to roll her eyes.

19 MISSED CONNECTIONS

L. F. Wade International Airport, Bermuda, the next day...

Donna was happy to be getting off the island. She drew a few nervous stares from some of her fellow passengers as she was escorted by two constables to the jetway entrance where her handcuffs were removed.

"Thanks for the lift, fellas."

The taller of the two constables said, "Just remember, if you ever try to come back to Bermuda again, you'll be staying a long while in our jail."

She nodded. "Take a good look at me, because it's the last time you'll ever see this face here." With that, she walked on toward the door of the plane.

The two constables waited by the jetway until the plane's door was closed, it was pushed back and had begun taxiing out for takeoff. Then they turned and left.

Inside the plane, Donna settled into her middle seat. The window was occupied by a young man in his twenties that was absorbed by the screen in front of him. She looked over at the guy on the aisle seat and saw gauze wraps sticking out beyond the cuffs of his long sleeve shirt. Something about his face was familiar...

Presley knew the job had to be finished, there was just too much at stake to leave the last two. Hell, he'd already risked everything including his own life, and if he was going to completely capitalize on all his planning and work, Morgan and Monroe had to go as well. He heard they had already flown back to the States when the ship left without them. Now the problem was that he didn't know where they lived and didn't yet have an idea about how to find them. He was hoping the cruise ship company might help him with that, but it wasn't like he had a lot of leverage with them if they didn't want to. The group's dinner boat had been arranged for privately, and the cruise line had picked up the tab for his hotel room last night as well as his plane fare. This was all probably a bit of goodwill to help stem any possibility of a lawsuit.

He was still running everything through his mind when some klutz bumped her legs against his while she was getting into her middle seat, causing him excruciating pain. The idiot was clueless as to what she'd done and was now busy checking out the young guy in the window seat. Presley was just going back to his thoughts when...

"Hey! You're the guy who lived through the boat explosion! Preston, right?" She put her hand out to shake his.

"Presley, but yes, that's me."

"Wow, you are one lucky fellow."

He studied her face. "You were on the cruise too. Why didn't you go back to the States on the ship?"

"Uh, I was in jail. They detained me thinking I had something to do with the bomb, but then they figured out I didn't. Then there was this other thing, which was really nothing, but they decided to deport me over it."

"Drugs?"

"No. I kind of locked my friend in his stateroom. They said I falsely imprisoned him." She made air quotes around the words "falsely imprisoned."

"What, did you lock your boyfriend out of your room?"

"Um, no, I locked my friend *in* his room. He's not my boyfriend, at least not yet. But that's only a matter of time."

This broad is wacko, he thought. "So, how do you lock someone in a cabin from the outside?"

"Epoxy." She smiled, being very proud of herself.

"Wow." He acted like he was impressed, but he was suddenly much warier of her.

"Yeah. Though I probably saved his life, his and his niece's. They were supposed to be on that boat with you. Hey, why didn't you get blown to bits like everybody else on it?"

She's as subtle as a baseball bat to the head, he thought. "I was up on the bow, about as far away from the fuel tank as you could get. Blew me out ahead and to the side. Everybody else was back by the stern where the bench seats and the flat deck part were. I just got burned." He pulled up a shirt sleeve and one pant leg.

"Wow. Lucky."

"Yes. I mean, I'm still alive, but I guess I'll be dealing with survivor's guilt for the rest of my life. And my ears are still ringing."

"I bet they are."

Presley said, "So it was Morgan and Monroe that you glued into their cabin. Lucky for them."

"Yeah. I'm thinking I might have had some kind of subliminal premonition. You'd have thought they would've been grateful, but they didn't even come to visit me while I was in jail."

Wow, this one is way off the rails. "Well, that was inconsiderate of them."

"Exactly what I thought, Preston."

"Presley."

"Whatever. Anyway, I'm going to let Sandy know that when I stay with him."

"Oh. You're on your way to Sandy's place?"

"That's the plan."

"Where does he live?"

"He moved out of *Bayside Estates*. I think he's on his boat somewhere over on ESVA."

"ESVA?"

"The Eastern Shore of Virginia."

"Oh. What, does he have his own dock on ESVA?"

"Wouldn't you if you were him?"

"I guess it would make sense. Although, his books are all about different marinas and the people that live in them. I thought for sure he lived in one."

"Well, maybe. I went to the ones that are owned by his fishing buddies, but I couldn't find either his boat or him. Missed him by a day at *Mallard Cove Marina* after they weighed in a big tuna the night before. It was in the next day's paper. I went there, but I couldn't find him or the sport fisherman he had been on."

"So how do you plan on finding him?"

"Well, he flew out after the ship left, and that means his stuff is still aboard. Somebody is going to show up and claim it, so I'll just follow them. He's going to be so happy that I found him again."

"Oh, I'll bet."

"So, what's on your agenda today," Sandy asked Betsy over breakfast at the *Cove* deck.

"I've been meaning to tell you, but with so much going on, I never got around to it. I'm flying back to Palm Beach this morning. I have a pending deal on my house, and I need to sign the papers. The real estate market down there is hot."

"I'll say, that was quick. But why not have the papers overnighted up here instead?"

"Well, I figured I'd have my annual physical with my old doctor while I'm down there. You know, one last visit before I have to go shopping for a new doctor up here. I was able to grab a cancellation spot."

"When will you be back?"

"Tomorrow night. Maybe we can have dinner?"

"Plan on it."

Betsy hated lying to Sandy, saying it was only a physical instead of trying to get to the root cause of some pain she'd been having. But she didn't want to worry him unnecessarily. She was sure it would turn out to be nothing...

"Maybe I could catch a ride with you? Sandy and I never got a chance to sit down and talk. We were planning on doing that on the return leg," Presley lied. He and Donna were riding on an airport shuttle, heading from Norfolk International to the cruise ship terminal satellite parking lot.

Donna replied, "I don't see why not. It's not like you're a stranger; we were on the ship together and we both are friends of Sandy's. He'll be so excited to see us."

"I bet. The cruise ship office said we could pick up our things after two p.m., so if we're lucky we'll run into him then."

They picked up Donna's car at the satellite lot a little before two, then drove over to the terminal's drop-off area. It turned out not to have any parking out in front except for the VIP lot across the street.

Presley said, "I'll run get our things, you keep circling here until you see me back at the curb."

He went into the terminal and found the unclaimed baggage area, which was almost deserted. The ship was in turnaround mode, having docked a few hours earlier and the crew was busy checking in the new passengers. He found both his and Donna's luggage. He'd disposed of the box of books he'd used to smuggle the bomb components and the torch aboard back in Bermuda, in a dumpster on the wharf. He saw two other bags tagged "Sanford Morgan" and "Micah Monroe" along with several cardboard boxes. All had originally been marked: "Deliver to *Mallard Cove Marina Dockmaster*." But that had been crossed off and replaced with, "*Hold For Pickup*."

He quickly left, flagging down Donna. He put both their bags in her trunk after removing his tablet and then joined her up front. "Looks like you were right, Donna. Their bags were there. They're marked for pickup, but originally they were supposed to be delivered to *Mallard Cove Marina*."

"I *knew* it! They were hiding him over there all along."

A horn sounded behind Donna's car, and she pulled away from the curb just in time to see Micah in the crosswalk thirty yards in front of her.

"I don't know if Micah's still sore over the whole epoxy thing. If it was Sandy, I'd go right up to him. But I think we might be better off just following Micah instead."

Presley said, "That's probably wise."

Micah disappeared in the terminal and Donna made the four-minute loop back around.

When they approached the area again, they saw Micah had pulled an SUV up to the curb. She was tipping a crewman who had loaded the bags and boxes into the back. Donna slowed, giving Micah time to get back in and pull away from the curb. Then she followed at a discreet distance, letting a car merge in between them as they got out onto the road. Micah was making a beeline for the CBBT, obviously heading back to ESVA.

"By the way, what do you mean, 'they were hiding him'? Were you talking about at the marina?"

"Yes! Remember, I told you I'd been there the day after they weighed in that big tuna. He was probably out fishing again, and that's why I couldn't find him or the boat he'd been on. It'll be handy having you with me; you can do the footwork when we get there."

"What footwork?"

"Finding out exactly where Sandy is, so I can go straight from the car to him. The management kind of told me not to come back again. But if you spot Sandy, I can get him to clear it all up with them, letting them know that it's okay and that I'm with him."

This was a complication that Presley hadn't expected, and one that he couldn't afford. Now if he was spotted with Donna, he'd probably be "tarred with the same brush." He had decided on the plane that at some point he'd need to get rid of her permanently; he couldn't leave any loose ends that could tie him to what was about to happen to them. Now that timetable for disposing of Donna would have to be moved up. Too bad for her.

Presley pulled up *Mallard Cove's* website on his tablet, studying the layout. The place was big, a large marina with four restaurants, a hotel, bait shop, charter boat row, and an in-and-out boat dry storage barn. He figured the hotel would be a perfect place to stay tonight while observing Morgan and Monroe's comings and goings from there as he formulated a plan.

Deputy Linton hadn't counted on the traffic jam on I-64. What was it about big-city drivers that they couldn't all keep going at the same pace? He'd flown into Richmond since it was cheaper and had a better flight schedule. But now because of the slowdown as he approached the tidewater area, he was behind schedule. He was worried he might miss DuBois at the Norfolk airport.

Arriving forty-five minutes late, he did indeed miss Donna, who was already on that airport shuttle van with Peterson. He figured there was a chance the boat had sailed from Bermuda with her bags still aboard, so he got back in his rental car and had the GPS direct him to the cruise ship terminal. Once again, he was a few minutes too late to catch her.

By the time he arrived, Donna was already on the CBBT, heading for ESVA. Unfortunately for him, he had no idea what she was driving, or where she would be going next. It was time to check in with the locals, so he headed to Norfolk Police Department on the off chance that they might have any information on DuBois. They didn't, so he asked for a recommendation for a cheap but decent motel. After he got settled, he had a call to make to his sheriff that he wasn't looking forward to making.

Micah did go straight to *Mallard Cove*, but she didn't head to any of the regular parking lots. Instead, she took the access driveway that led past the hotel, the back of the bait shop, and finally the in-and-out boat barn. Donna had to lag way back to avoid being spotted. When they finally crept up beyond the boat barn, Micah's car had disappeared. Donna drove around the barn, searching for the car, but it wasn't between the barn and the water where the drive ended.

"What the heck! She can't have vaporized," she said.

Presley suppressed a chuckle since that was exactly what he had originally planned for her on the boat in Bermuda. "Wait, what's that over there," he said, pointing out a motorized gate in the tree line that marked the end of the property.

Donna pulled up by it, staying just far enough back to avoid a security camera that covered the driveway area by a keypad. They couldn't see beyond the gate, due to some strategically placed evergreens. Another, smaller gate was beside it, with a dark concrete walkway leading through it. A similar bunch of evergreens blocked any view beyond it as well.

A man came around the side of the boat barn, staring at the car. Presley said, "We need to get out of here, we're drawing attention. Drive back to the bait shack."

"Why there?"

"Because they'll know if he's out fishing or not, and I can pull up the satellite view of this place on my tablet."

Donna nodded, "Good thinking."

She parked behind the bait shop, just off the access road as Presley said, "Wait here, I'll be right back."

Five minutes later he was back in the car with a small bag. Donna ignored the bag, figuring it was a small purchase to avoid suspicion while he asked questions.

"So, what did they say?"

"You're right, he's out fishing, and won't be back until dark. We'll have to kill some time until then."

In reality, he hadn't asked about Sandy at all, not wanting anyone to recall that and make the connection between the two later. Now he was focused on his tablet, having pulled up a satellite picture of the entire property and the area beyond the tree line. He let out a low whistle.

Donna asked, "What is it?"

"There's no wonder why you couldn't find Sandy and his boat. Look at this." He handed over his tablet which showed the details of *Casey's Cove,* and all the boat slips it contained.

"This looks like the stealthiest way we can approach Sandy's is from over by this public boat ramp on the state park property. It looks like there's a way we could hike from that little parking area through the woods to the back of this building by the pool," Presley said. He was pointing to an adjacent state park area that bordered the *Virginia Inside Passage*, which he hoped wasn't busy now during the work-week. "See? There's a road back into there about a half mile down from the *Mallard Cove* entrance. Let's go look."

Donna drove out onto the main road, making her turn less than a minute later as the map had shown. There was a small maze of old, worn-out, asphalt roads that wove themselves back into the empty woods. Presley called out her turns as he studied their location on the tablet map. A few minutes later they pulled up to the smaller of the two parking areas. As he had hoped, both were deserted.

"Are you sure this is a good idea, Preston?"

"It's Presley, and yes, I do. There isn't any way in from that boat barn side, and we can't just hang around there, you saw the way that guy looked us over. I imagine they must keep a close eye on that place. Did you see the size of that yacht in the overhead? I'm willing to bet that camera at the gate isn't the only security they have."

"Do you think that big yacht is Sandy's? That's where he lives?" Donna could already picture herself on it, living there without a care in the world. A perfect, made-in-her-mind dream world.

"It would stand to reason that it is. He has made a ton of money, especially from Hollywood. And from what you said, his people aren't going to let you near him. The only possible way you'll get to him is by cutting through these woods and climbing over that back fence. Hopefully, it isn't that high."

"Doesn't matter, I'll climb it. Let's go."

Donna was so excited and intent on getting to Sandy, that she missed seeing that Presley brought along the bag from the bait shop. She led the way, focused on what was in front of her, not what he was doing behind her. He pulled a pair of orange cotton fishing gloves with checkerboard patterned rubber nonslip out of the bag and put them on. Next, he pulled out a plastic-handled boning knife. Moving up quickly behind her, he reached around and grabbed her chin, yanking her head to the left. With his other hand, he reached around her other side and drove the boning knife up between her ribs and into her heart. As she slumped down to the ground he said, "For the last time, my name is Presley, not Preston."

Her body fell on her left side and then rolled onto her back. Presley carefully took her hand and wrapped it around the handle of the knife, which was still lodged in her chest, leaving only her fingerprints on it. This looked like a suicide by an obsessed, mentally deranged fan, leaving herself as a sacrifice to the object of her attention, as close to him as she was able to get. He took the car keys out of her pocket and left her where she'd fallen.

Fortunately, the ground was hard, and he'd not left any footprints. He doubled back to the car, adjusting the seat to fit him, and drove to the *Mallard Cove Hotel*. Removing the gloves before going and checking in, he took his bag up to his room. Then he put the gloves on again before driving the car back over to the same parking lot and readjusting the seat to where he'd found it. He left the key in the ignition and the driver's door open to entice anyone who might be a curious passerby or to invite any potential joyriders. Then he hiked through the woods over to the tree line behind the hotel. He peered out from the woods to make sure the coast was clear before emerging from the trees. Then it was time to go over to the beach bar for the afternoon; he needed a few drinks and an alibi.

20 TOO MANY COINCIDENCES

"Hey, Sandy, I hear you're retiring."

Casey had come over to *C2* for a swim and found Sandy by himself in a chaise lounge on the pool deck. Almost by himself that is, since KC was curled up on a chair beside him.

"Not retiring, Casey, retired. Past tense. Done."

"Congratulations. So, what are you going to do with all that extra time you'll have now?"

"I'm planning on doing more fishing; hopefully a lot of it with Betsy."

"Nice! I hope fishing more with me can also fit into that schedule."

"Count on it."

"Hey, *Steel Leader* is on her way back south, so Eric, Missy, Candi, Dawn, and I are taking her out for a demo day tomorrow. You and Betsy want to join us?"

"You know I'd normally jump at the chance, but Betsy went down to Florida this morning, and she's coming back tomorrow. We have dinner plans, and I don't want to mess with those."

Casey nodded. "Sounds like you have your priorities in the proper order. She's quite a nice person."

"That she is. Don't know exactly what she sees in me, but whatever it is, I'm glad she does. She got an instant KC seal of approval, too. That doesn't happen much."

"Tell me about it! I'm only occasionally able to pet him, even after feeding him a pound of tuna bites."

Hearing his name, KC opened one eye long enough to glare at Casey for interrupting his nap, then closed it and went back to sleep.

"Do you have dinner plans tonight as well?"

Sandy shook his head. "No. To tell you the truth, I haven't thought beyond cocktail hour yet."

"Good, then you're free to join us on *Lady Dawn*. Eric and crew are due in any time now."

"I'll take you up on that, thanks. I'm minus a boat-mate these days, and it's kind of quiet around there now."

"Yeah, I heard about that. I'm happy for those kids. Sounds like a nice house they found up on the way to Cape Charles."

"I haven't seen it yet, but at least they'll have some privacy by being out of here and living by themselves. Nice to see them both so happy."

Carl Linton returned to his hotel room after dinner just as his cell phone started ringing. He saw the number had a Norfolk area code.

"Linton."

"Deputy? Sergeant Caruso at Norfolk PD, we met this afternoon?"

"Yeah. What can I do for you, Sergeant?"

"We've had a little luck in your search for the DuBois woman. You might call it dumb luck. A couple of kids from up on the Shore just led one of our units on a wild chase through our town. They crashed the car they were in, and the temp tags on it were registered to your suspect. Her suitcase and clothes were found in the trunk. Said they 'found' the car abandoned in the state park over on ESVA. The Sheriff's Department over there searched the area and discovered a body.

An apparent self-inflicted stab wound to the chest. I'm sending you a picture now for an ID."

Linton's phone pinged, and he brought up the picture. It was the Donna DuBois he'd talked to that day a few months ago at her farm. But like so many things with her, something didn't feel right.

"That's her, Sergeant. But let me ask you something. How many people have you heard about who committed suicide by stabbing themselves in the chest?"

"Including this one?"

"Yeah."

"One."

Presley had deliberately gotten into an argument with a guy at the bar, drawing the attention of the wait staff and the manager who advised both of them to quiet down. Then the guy told him that there were no hard feelings, and Presley was welcome to buy him a beer.

He was tempted to tell the guy to shove it, but since he seemed to be well known and mostly liked by the staff and the regulars, he did buy him that beer, and three more after it. He turned out to be a charter boat captain and one of the stars on some cable show about tuna fishing. The regulars and staff all called him "Baloney."

As Presley sat at the bar listening to Baloney talk about himself, he noticed three police cars coming over Fisherman Inlet Bridge with their lights on. He thought that if they were related to that DuBois woman, his alibi timing couldn't have been any better. He smiled and asked Baloney if he needed another beer.

The next morning Sandy was seated at his usual breakfast table on the deck of the *Cove*. He was reading in the *ESVA Telegraph* about the body of a suicide victim that had been found somewhere just beyond C2 last night. Police had identified the middle-aged woman from out of state but weren't releasing her name until after notification of her family.

"Sandy? Hey! What are the chances of meeting you here!"

Sandy looked up and recognized Presley Peterson. "Hey, Presley. Better than you might think since I live here."

"I didn't know that! Hey, mind if I sit down?"

Ordinarily, he would mind, especially since he didn't particularly like the guy, but he felt sorry for him after he'd gotten burned in that explosion. He motioned to the empty seat across from him. Thinking he only wanted to catch up over coffee, he became even more irritated when Presley ordered a full breakfast. The server filled his coffee cup before going to put in his order.

"I hear they have the best breakfast on ESVA here."

Sandy nodded. "If not, it's one of the best."

"So, have you heard any more from the police in Bermuda about the bombing?"

"I figured you would have, Presley."

For a split second, Presley stopped his cup halfway up to his mouth. "What do you mean by that?"

His reaction struck Sandy as strange. "Well, you're the one who survived but was hurt; it's only logical that they would keep you informed of any developments, especially if you're needed to go back to testify."

"Oh. Right. Yeah, I haven't heard anything yet."

Sandy watched as two uniformed officers walked up the stairs and were greeted by Mimi. To his surprise, she led them over to his table.

"This is Sandy." She motioned to him.

"Mr. Morgan, I'm Deputy Ortiz of Northampton County, and this is Deputy Linton."

"What can I do for you?"

"We're investigating the death of a woman named Donna DuBois. I understand you had some problems with her recently on a Bermuda cruise?"

"Please sit down, gentlemen, you're catching me by surprise.

Donna DuBois is *dead*? What happened to her?" When Sandy saw them looking at Presley he said, "This is Presley Peterson, another writer who was also on that same cruise."

"We aren't quite sure and won't know until after the autopsy is performed. Originally it appeared that she may have taken her own life, but now we aren't so certain of that. Deputy Linton is here from out of town and had wanted to talk to her as a person of interest in three potential homicides, but obviously, that's no longer possible."

Sandy noticed the color drain from Presley's face, and he wondered what was behind that. "No, I guess not. But what does this have to do with me?"

Linton spoke. "What was your involvement with DuBois? Did she ever mention the deaths of her husband and son or her old boyfriend?"

Sandy paused then said, "Not to speak ill of the dead but most of our interactions were about me trying to get rid of her. No, she never mentioned any family. Frankly, we never got that deep into a conversation. She seemed to be in her own little world." He went on to tell them about his interactions with her.

"That matches up with what the Bermuda PD told us. What about you, Mr. Peterson, did you have any conversations with her?"

"I saw her on the cruise and after the bathroom incident, all the writers had heard about her. Frankly though, after the explosion, everything was mostly a blur. I came over here to get away and do a life reset and forget all that."

Ortiz said, "So, you're here on ESVA as a guest of Mr. Morgan?"

"I had no idea that he lived here. It was a coincidence that I ran into him a few minutes ago. I'm staying in that hotel." He motioned toward the *Mallard Cove Hotel*.

Linton gave Ortiz a quick sideways glance but said nothing. Cops aren't big believers in coincidences. Sandy saw the glance, and also thought it was strange that Peterson had shown up here, but for now, he kept quiet.

"Well, thank you both for your cooperation. We'll be in touch if we have any further questions. If you'd both please write your phone numbers down." He passed a small notepad over to Peterson.

"Sorry, my phone was destroyed in the explosion, and I haven't gotten around to replacing it yet."

Linton said, "When you do, it'll be the same number, so if you wouldn't mind..."

Reluctantly, Presley wrote down a number and passed the notebook to Sandy.

Ortiz said, "Thank you both for your cooperation. We'll be in touch."

After they left, a worried-looking Presley said, "How did we go from being 'in touch' if they had more questions to definitely being contacted again?"

Sandy wondered where this was coming from. "I don't know and frankly I don't care if they contact me. It's not like I had anything more to do with her after I left Bermuda. Just a strange coincidence, her dying on ESVA."

Presley's eyes bulged, "How did you know she died over here?"

Once again Sandy saw something about Presley that was a little off. As a writer, Sandy was more attuned to words than most people, and Presley had just asked him how "did" he know something rather than how "do" you know it. Saying "did," implied that Presley had known about it beforehand. Sandy held up his newspaper, "We don't get many suicides or murders around here. It had to be Donna."

Relieved, Presley said, "Oh, that makes sense."

Presley's breakfast arrived just as Sandy got a cryptic text from Betsy saying that she had to stay longer in Florida, and that she wouldn't be able to make dinner. No explanation, and no estimated return time. Without a doubt, she was a very independent woman who didn't have to report to him, but usually breaking a dinner date came with a more detailed explanation. Especially since he could've gone out fishing on *Steel Leader* with Casey and crew since she wouldn't be back this evening.

"Something wrong, Sandy?" Presley had looked up from his food.

"Huh? Oh, it's nothing. Hey, enjoy your breakfast and your stay on ESVA. I've got to run." He stood up.

"Oh, well maybe we can get together later today? Perhaps for a drink?"

"Sorry, Presley, I've got a full schedule. Maybe some other time."

With that, Sandy left. Presley bristled at what was an obvious brush-off. It made him that much more determined to dispatch Sandy, even though it would happen so close to DuBois's death. He didn't like those cops knowing that he was in such close proximity to where DuBois was found and that he'd had breakfast with Sandy. But he had no choice, he had to move forward if he was to capitalize on being the sole surviving author from that cruise. He needed to get working on his book about the experience, and the mystery behind it. The timing was everything.

First, he'd focus on Sandy, then he'd have to deal with Micah. Unless... yes, that could work. An automobile accident—a two-for-one. He smiled to himself as he went back to his breakfast, one of the best he'd ever had.

"Fishing from this boat is fantastic, Dad! She's so stable."

Steel Leader had captured Missy's heart. As far as she was concerned, this boat was the ultimate fishing machine. At least it would be until *Sharke* was launched.

Eric agreed. "One very stable platform. Of course, it's not as rough today as it was the last time we were out, but you'd still feel it a lot more on *Predator* today. No offense, Casey."

Casey smiled, "None taken. It's why I was drooling over that hull down at Jarrett Bay. You couldn't be on a more stable platform if you were fishing from a barge, and we got out here in half the time.

"You should go up to the bridge and check out that Furuno sonar, it's amazing. The captain told me that he had spotted your yellowfin tuna that day, Missy. He'd seen it coming up behind *Predator* in our bait spread, so there wasn't anything he could've done about it by that point. But if it had passed on our baits, he'd have been able to track it and get out in front and maybe have a shot at catching it. There's no substitute for having the right equipment."

Eric and Missy climbed the ladder to the massive flybridge where Jeff, Candi, Dawn, and Micah were all seated, talking and watching the baits in their wake. Casey had Jeff ask Micah at the last minute, wanting to give the two of them some fishing time together. As they watched, *Steel Leader*'s captain was demonstrating the various features of the Furuno when he suddenly yelled, "Get ready! I've got a pod of fish coming up behind us."

Missy almost slid down the ladder to get to the rods. As she stepped down from the mezzanine deck, two outrigger clips snapped, followed closely by a third. Casey, Missy, and the mate each picked up a rod and started reeling until the lines came tight. Suddenly the surface of the ocean erupted as three white marlin thrashed and leaped, trying to rid themselves of the hooks.

Candi had joined Casey and Missy in the cockpit, and the mate passed her his rod. The next fifteen minutes were a fire drill, with lines crossing and anglers switching sides trying to keep from losing their fish. All three fish were released after the mate held their stiff, pointed bills while he removed the circle hooks from the corners of their mouths. He did bring both Missy's and Candi's fish on board just long enough to snap quick pictures with them, then those fish were also released unharmed.

"My first white marlin of the season," Missy beamed.

"And plenty more to come." Eric had also joined them. "This boat is amazing. I can't wait until ours is finished and up here."

"Another couple of months. Looooong months," Casey said with a wry grin.

"And a lot of helicopter rides down to Jarrett Bay in the meantime," said Eric.

"Oh, twist my arm." Casey loved anything that flew, especially that Sikorsky.

21 ANOTHER BOOK

Betsy's strange-sounding text bothered Sandy all day long. Yes, she was independent, and no, they had no formal relationship or obligation to each other. But this wasn't like her, at least what Sandy knew of her.

He spent the day puttering around his boat and even began to question his decision to retire. With Micah now moved out, Betsy down in Florida, and the rest of the *Casey's Cove* crew busy working or out on the boat demo, he was experiencing something for the first time since that period right after his wife died; listlessness.

He thought about going over to one of the beach bars, but two things stopped him. The first was the possibility of running into that Presley character. The guy had begun to creep him out. The second reason was it would be too easy to slide into the habit of becoming a barfly. He'd seen that sedentary lifestyle adopted by far too many retirees back in the Keys.

No, his whole idea about retiring was to become more active and see more of the world around him. What he needed was the right equipment, so he went online to see what outboards were available in his area. He chuckled to himself as he thought this must be partly what was meant by the term, "retail therapy."

Sandy was surprised by both the number and the variety of the boats that were for sale. As he went from listing to listing, he couldn't help but wonder why some of them were for sale. Moving up or moving down in size? Death in the family? Divorce? Costs much more to maintain than they ever dreamed? He knew that so often this was the case. People forgot or weren't aware of the ten percent rule: the one that said you needed to plan on spending ten percent of a boat's purchase price annually for its upkeep.

With some of the more interesting listings, he couldn't help but dream up backstories. He had a writer's soul, and this came with the territory. As he looked up and out the salon window, he was surprised to see that night had already started falling. Then he had another surprise when there was a knock on the cabin door.

After breakfast, Presley scoped out the marina and the rest of the *Mallard Cove* operation. Then he slipped over to an old gravel access road beyond the tree line behind the hotel. He'd crossed this weed-choked road after he ditched Donna's car and noted that it led toward that mini-marina complex where Morgan lived. He followed it now, finding that it had been abandoned after the construction was completed. A low hog wire fence and some bushes now cut across it. In the distance, he saw a one-story structure.

Climbing over the fence, he cautiously made his way over toward the building, discovering it was an oversized pool house. Fortunately, the place was deserted, and he continued past it toward a helicopter pad with a large private helicopter parked in the center. Beyond that was a seaplane ramp that dumped into the *Virginia Inside Passage*. To the right was that small marina basin. He crept over to the marina's bulkhead, taking care to look for anyone who might be about. But still, there was no one in sight.

Scanning the names on the two boat sterns that he could see, the big yacht was the *Lady Dawn*, which didn't sound like it would be connected to Morgan. The stern of the last boat over next to a boathouse bore the name *Epilogue*. Bingo! That had to be Morgan's. Now that he knew where to find him, Presley went back to the *Cove Beach Bar* for an early but extended lunch and a couple of beers spread out over the next several hours. Finally, around dusk he paid his bill in cash, leaving a nominal tip, wanting to be remembered for being there, but not for the exact time he left.

Sandy opened the cabin door, surprised to find Presley on his back deck.

"How the hell did you get through the security gate?"

"Uh, I hitched a ride on a service cart thingy. The fellow who's driving it tol' me where your boat was." It was all a lie of course, but one designed to put him at ease. He purposely slurred his speech a bit, and his breath still smelled of beer. It was all part of his plan.

KC looked over from his spot on the couch and instantly went into a "Halloween cat" stance, his back arched and his fur standing on end. He was hissing, spitting, and growling in Presley's direction. This was even more agitated than he'd been that day when they passed by the Hampton Roads Bridge Tunnel. He leaped up onto the flat dash area in front of the lower helm station, backing into the corner, now crouched down and still growling. Sandy looked from him back to Presley, who had now stepped into the salon.

"Cats don' like me much, an' the feelin's mutual. I'm more uva dog guy. Can I use the head, 'cause I really gotta whiz, ya knowhatImean?"

Worried about the possible consequences if he didn't allow it, Sandy directed him down the steps to the crew's head. Instead, Presley lurched into his stateroom, presumably to use that en suite head. It had been a ruse designed to allow him to look and see if anyone was up in the vacant forward spaces, and then to search for something in Sandy's cabin. He found it in the first place he looked.

As Presley started back up the darkened corridor, Sandy yelled, "Hey, you forgot to flush!" His motorized vintage marine toilet made enough racket to wake the dead. That's when he saw the pistol in

Presley's hand. He recognized it as his own, the one from the night-stand next to his bunk.

"Hey Morgan, do you know the percentage of liveaboards who keep a loaded firearm within an arm's reach of their bunk? I do. Because I always do my research before I write a book. That's why mine are so good." Gone was any hint of inebriation in his voice or manner.

Sandy instantly understood this was something that had been planned, it wasn't a spur-of-the-moment thing. He also knew what he said and did next would set the tone for how this was going to play out. "What do you mean 'books,' as in plural? You've only got one, and it isn't that good."

Presley smiled. "It is, and much better researched than your drivel. And as far as plural, I've been laying out the plot for my next one for months. It's about the sole survivor of a cursed author cruise, which of course would be me. And I already would have been if it hadn't been for your interfering little chicky and her tube of glue."

The realization hit him like a wind gust, "The boat explosion... that was you?"

"You know, for an old guy, you still catch on fast."

"But why?"

"Because this is the best advertising. Much better than any of those promotion platforms they are, or were, all fond of using. And it will probably land me a deal with one of those big publishing houses, maybe even the one you write for."

"Wrote. I retired yesterday."

"Ah, too bad. A day late, and a dollar short. You could've had a nice long retirement if you'd have never gotten on that cruise."

"So, you killed Donna, too."

"She was getting to be such a bother and could've gotten in the way of my meeting plans with you and your niece."

"You were riding around here with her." More of a statement than a question.

"Yes. She wasn't going to stop hounding you, by the way. She was completely infatuated with you. Honestly, I thought about letting that play itself out. I figured once you rejected her, she'd have been likely to do a murder-suicide thing, but I just couldn't leave it all to chance. Too risky."

Sandy said, "But you weren't aware until this morning that she was wanted for questioning in three murders."

"I know, right? She seemed like such a gentle, but misguided soul. Quite a plot twist, I think I'll use that one in the future." He grinned. "Okay, time to go."

"Where are we going?"

"To pay a little visit to your niece. Where is she, by the way?"

"At her house in Virginia Beach, but why would you expect me to take you there?"

"Because even without your help I'm going to find her. There are easy and humane ways to go, and some that aren't so... nice. Think back on the most vicious way you've ever killed a woman in your books, then take it three steps beyond that. Is this what you want for your niece?" The look he gave Sandy said he meant every single word. "Now, take your phone out of your pocket and leave it on the couch. I don't want the cops to be able to track us."

The two walked slowly in the dark over to Sandy's truck. He kept looking around for help, but the dimly lit docks were deserted. He climbed into the driver's seat while Presley kept his gun pointed at him as he went around to the passenger's side. Sandy had already formulated a plan in his head. He'd given Presley the wrong location for Micah's house on purpose. There was no way he was going to let someone who had murdered almost two dozen people get anywhere near his niece, no matter what it would cost him. Presley was as crazy as Donna, but his was a deep-rooted insanity that he was able to mask from view. There was only one way for Sandy to be certain that Micah would continue to be safe from this madman.

As they pulled out onto US 13 heading south onto the CBBT, Fisherman Inlet Bridge quickly rose in front of them. Sandy smoothly but rapidly accelerated to just over eighty-five miles per hour before they reached the top. Presley suddenly realized how fast they were going.

"Hey, slow down old man, I don't want to get pulled over for speed... ungh." Presley was thrown against the door as Sandy turned the wheel hard over to the left, the truck almost going up on two tires.

Fisherman Inlet Bridge is actually two separate two-lane bridges, built in two different decades, about thirty feet apart. The side guardrails on the bridges are made of three separate, six-inch horizontal metal tubes. They are only designed to deflect a vehicle that hits them at a glancing blow. But they couldn't dissipate all the energy transferred during an almost directly perpendicular hit, which was exactly what Sandy planned.

The thin-walled tubing parted with the impact, the truck plunging over the side in that gap between the bridges. Falling forty feet down toward the watery blackness, he realized he was about to land in the very thing that had most terrified him his entire life. But right now, he was strangely calm, knowing he had saved Micah, though he regretted leaving Betsy behind. Though he knew his late wife was waiting for him just beyond that inky black surface below.

22 THE VISIT

The ride back was as spectacular as both the sunset ahead of them and the day's fishing behind them. Casey and Eric's group were all as excited now for the new boat as they'd ever been. This had been such a great opportunity to experience a day on a boat almost identical to their new one. This also gave them ideas for several tweaks and changes to be done to *Sharke.*

Casey told the *Steel Leader* crew that dinner and drinks were on him at the *Cove.* They were docking there overnight before continuing south in the morning. The captain slowed to idle speed about five minutes out to let the bearings on the turbos have a chance to cool down. About thirty yards out from the inlet jetties, Missy yelled and pointed over in the direction of Fisherman Inlet Bridge.

"A car! It just went over the bridge! I saw the lights and then the splash!"

The captain quickly turned the big sport fisherman in the direction of the span. On the FLIR screen, the infrared display showed something about a foot high floating on the surface of the channel, but it quickly disappeared. The captain asked Jeff, "What's my clearance and depth up there?"

"Forty feet vertical, and fifteen feet depth. The current is ripping out of the bay, so whatever it is should be moving in this direction, well clear of the bridge." He knew that the car wouldn't be standing still in this current as it sank.

"Good. With our antennas up, that clearance would be marginal." The captain lowered the Furuno sonar periscope and powered it up. Even several hundred yards away, they could make out the pilings from the bridge and its fenders, and a large object which was moving toward them as it slowly sank toward the bottom.

Micah asked, "Do you have a diving mask?"

Casey added, "Two of them?"

The mate replied he'd get them from below. The captain turned on the high-intensity underwater lights, then called the Coast Guard to advise them of the situation. The lights were designed to attract fish when they were out fishing, as well as garner attention when they were docked. The fifteen-foot depth was about the limit for the bright lights to penetrate in this slightly murky bay water.

The captain warned, "That's going to be a tough current."

Jeff said proudly, "She's a Keys Conch."

He nodded. "'Nuff said."

Micah hurried down to the cockpit with Casey where they unloaded their pockets. The mate handed them each a mask as well as a large metal chisel from the boat's tools. "In case you have to break the side windows."

The captain called out, "We're directly over it. Make sure you surface well clear of the props and shafts because I'm going to be in and out of gear to keep our position. Go!"

Casey and Micah both rolled over backward off the covering boards, each surfacing to get a breath, then diving down. The murky brownish water was a little cloudier than it had looked from the surface. But the Furuno had nailed it, and the vehicle was directly beneath them, lying on the passenger side.

In the spill of the boat's lights, they could see the front of what had been a pickup truck was demolished. But even after impacting the surface of the water, the cab windows were still intact. Casey spotted a waterline creeping upward on the windshield glass as the remaining air slowly escaped. He motioned "up" to Micah, and the two surfaced off to the side of the boat.

Casey said, "Not much air left in there, and as soon as we break that side window it'll all be gone. I'll try the door, but if it's jammed, you'll have to reach through the window, check for a seatbelt, and pull the driver out since you're skinnier than me. I think there's a passenger, too."

"Got it. Let's go."

The two descended again, this time going straight for the driver's door. Casey tried the handle, but it was either locked or jammed or both. He and Micah used the pointed end of their chisels on the window, and it shattered with the second set of blows. As they figured, all the remaining trapped air escaped in a rush. Casey reached in and tried the interior door handle. The lock disengaged and Micah helped him pull the door open. Casey reached across the man, unfastening the seatbelt, then pulled his limp body toward the surface.

Micah took Casey's place at the door, reaching across and unfastening the passenger's seatbelt while being careful herself not to get tangled in the deflated airbags. She tugged at his arm, but one of his feet had been jammed up under the dashboard. She pulled as hard as she could, but he wouldn't budge. By then her lungs were burning, and her vision started to narrow. She let go of the man's arm, backed out of the cab, and shot to the surface, just missing the chine of the boat above.

She looked around while taking two quick, deep breaths, but saw no sign of Casey or the first man. She dove down again, trying hard to free the man from the cab, but it was no use. Again, at the limit of her breath, she was forced to surface.

Dawn was waiting and watching for her. "Micah, get aboard, we have to get to shore!"

"No, there's still a person trapped in the cab."

"He'll have drowned by now, and we can still save Sandy, but we have to get him to shore!"

"Wait, what?"

"It was Sandy you two rescued, but we have to get him over to the paramedics, so get aboard!"

Dawn pulled her by the arms through the open transom door. Right in front of her Casey and Eric were performing CPR on her uncle, who was flat on his back on the deck. The boat's captain quickly turned *Steel Leader* and throttled up toward the *Mallard Cove* inlet a few hundred yards ahead. Dragging a huge stern wake into the marina with them, he then slid the big sportfish sideways up against the fuel dock. A rescue squad truck was backing in by the bulkhead.

The paramedics quickly evaluated Sandy, then placed him on a gurney and into the back of their van. They raced off to the hospital, with Micah and Jeff following in her car.

Soon the waterway offshore of the beach bars was crowded with boats with blue strobe lights. Both the Coast Guard as well as Northampton County Sheriff's deputies took statements from the passengers and crew of *Steel Leader*. A diver from the Sheriff's Department was finally able to free and recover Presley's body, then a buoy was attached to Sandy's truck so salvors could locate and raise it in the daylight.

Casey and the rest of the gang rushed into the waiting room, finding Jeff sitting alone.

"How's Sandy?"

Jeff said, "He's not breathing by himself. His lungs were full of water. He hacked some of it up and the rest they suctioned out. But now they're worried about those little sac things that put the oxygen into the bloodstream. Something about surfactant and getting washed off with saltwater. They've got him on a ventilator with oxygen, and he's sedated. If he doesn't develop an infection, they'll start weaning him off it in a day or so."

Dawn asked, "How did he end up going off the bridge?"

"No clue. He's been unconscious the whole time."

Micah came into the room and sat next to Jeff. "They'll only let me in for five minutes every hour. The doctor said that these next twenty-four hours are the critical period. If he doesn't develop an infection, we should see some improvement by then."

The mambo known as Mama Ceci leaned over Sandy, clucking her tongue. "Dese doctahs tink dey know it all, okay. Gat you here wit'out you gris-gris, dats no good. I brought a new one, jus' in case, okay?" She tied an amulet necklace around his neck that was identical to his first one. "You gwan be fine, Sandy Morgan, okay. Tho tings not gonna be like you tought or want, okay. You gwan get true dat as well. You a good man, and now my debt be paid bak, okay. Res' easy, Sandy."

An hour later Micah walked in and saw a noticeable improvement in Sandy's color. She also saw something that shocked her. She reached into her pocket and removed Sandy's amulet that the nurses had removed, then felt the one hanging around her neck. She stared at the identical one that now adorned Sandy's neck. While she wasn't sure exactly how it got there, she was going to make sure it stayed put.

The captain of Betsy's boat, *Cheri*, had come over to the Cove in search of Mimi. "Hi. My boss asked me to leave these with you, for Sandy Morgan. She hasn't been able to reach him."

"Yeah, he's in the hospital, he had a car wreck last night."

The captain winced. "I hope it's not serious."

"We all do." She looked down at the pair of keys he had just handed her. "What are these for?"

"Our outboard. She told me to leave it here until we get back, and she wants him to use it until she does."

"I thought you were here at least for the summer. Where are you headed?"

"Tampa."

She thought that was a strange direction to head as the summer heated up, but she said, "I'll see that he gets them."

"Thanks."

After he left, Mimi tried Betsy's number, but it went to voicemail. A minute later she got a text from her, *"Hi Meems, not quite up to talking. I guess you got the keys?"*

"Yes, I'll get them to Sandy when I can, but he was in an accident last night, and he's in the hospital."

"How bad was he hurt? Is he going to be all right?"

"He almost drowned. Went off the Fisherman Bridge in his truck. Lung issues so we won't know for a while if there'll be infections."

"Keep me in the loop, please."

"Will do. When are you coming back?"

"I don't know. As soon as I'm able if I'm able." There was a pause then, *"Don't want to worry Sandy, so keep that to yourself, please."*

"Will do."

"You've always been a good friend, Mimi, thank you for everything."

Mimi stared at the last line while she waited to see if Betsy would say anything more, but no other texts came. Now she was worried about two friends.

Four days later...

"So, he had the gun on you the entire time?" Detective Ortiz was questioning Sandy, who was well on the mend.

"Yes. And I had to keep him away from Micah, or we'd have both been dead."

"This was all over book sales?" He'd seen crimes committed over much smaller things, but this one was still on the bizarre side.

"Yes. He seemed to think that by killing off a bunch of those who he saw as his competition, he believed he could take the top spot in the ratings."

Micah added, "Here's the thing; everyone on that cruise and in our group all worked together. We all knew that we can only write so many books each year, so we tried to make sure that our readers were reading our friends' books after they finished our latest ones rather than buying from authors none of us knew. For whatever reason, he could never fully grasp that concept."

"Because he was a homicidal egomaniac, that's why. And a hack on top of it all." Sandy almost spat out the words.

"Well, this points our investigation in a whole new direction. And I'm sure the Bermuda PD will have a bunch of new questions for you as well."

"Then they can get their Bermudan butts over here because I'm not going back over there!"

Micah suppressed a smile. It was obvious Sandy was getting better since he was becoming more cantankerous.

"Hah. I'll pass that along, Mr. Morgan. I'm sure they'll be glad to fight each other over a stateside shopping trip paid for by their department."

"So, Betsy isn't back yet? Has anyone heard from her? They won't let me have my phone in here…"

Sandy's doctor came in, interrupting him. "Good news! We'll be releasing you tomorrow, Mr. Morgan."

"Better news, Doc, I'm leaving today. Micah, get my clothes."

The doctor frowned, "We want to keep you one more night, just to be safe."

"No, you want to keep me in here one more night so Medicare can make the next payment on your condo over at Wintergreen Ski Resort. I'm getting out of here. Micah, find my clothes or so help me I'll leave here bare-butt naked."

"Stop the car!" Sandy looked over from the driveway, down past the bait shop, and over toward the docks. "Where's *Cheri*?"

Micah hesitantly said, "It left a few days ago."

"Where did it go, and why didn't you tell me?"

"Tampa and we didn't want you to worry."

"Well, that didn't work. I'm worried. Why did it go to Tampa?"

"I'll let Betsy tell you. Mimi said she left you a text on your phone."

"Why... how did Mimi know that?"

"Betsy told her she was going to."

"What's it say?"

"We don't know."

"Get me to the boat."

"I'm sorry I wasn't there for you, Sandy. I hear you are on the mend, and I'm so happy about that. I wish I had good news to share from my end. During my physical, the doctor discovered I had a very aggressive form of cancer that was already well along. I just thought I'd wrenched my back on all those tuna we caught.

"I've come to the best cancer treatment center here in Tampa. There's a new chemo regimen they've developed that's currently in trials, and the good news is I'm included in it. But it's very tough, and takes its toll on the entire body, whether it's successful or not. I'm having my boat brought down so I have a comfortable and familiar place to rest in between treatments.

"I know you're thinking that you should come down here to be with me. I'm not going to ask you please not to come and not to call, I'm telling you not to do either. This chemo is kicking my tail, and I'm exhausted. I don't want anyone around except the private nurses I hired to take care of me on the boat.

"If all goes well, I should be back up there by the fall. I'm holding out hope that this will be the case. But if it's not, I'd like to ask you one last favor. Please take my ashes out to the canyon where we fished together and ask Mimi to go along as well. But I'm hopeful the next time we go out there together I'll be at the helm. You run the boat too damn slow."

Betsy

Sandy sat down heavily on the couch. Silently, he handed the phone to Micah as KC hopped up next to him and snuggled against his thigh. Every other time he'd done this he had started purring, but not today. Cats know things.

Sandy unconsciously reached up and rubbed the amulet between his fingers and thumb. He thought back to a dream he'd had in the hospital. One where the mambo that Micah met had visited him, and he recalled some of what he dreamed she'd said, *"You gwan be fine, Sandy Morgan, okay. Tho tings not gonna be like you tought or want, okay. You gwan get true dat as well."*

It was like the whole time since he'd gotten up here had been a dream, and she was another part of it. He looked up to Micah, who now had a tear running down one cheek. She saw him fingering the amulet, then pulled the original from her pocket.

He told her, "I thought it was all a dream or a byproduct of being sedated. She was there, and told me that things wouldn't turn out as I wanted, but that I'd get through it."

"One day at a time, Sandy."

EPILOGUE

Texts came from Betsy only sporadically over the next week and a half. Sandy was so tempted to ignore her wishes and fly to Tampa, but he respected her more than that. In her short final text, he could tell things weren't going well, and that she was so exhausted. His subsequent texts went unanswered. Then two days later he got the call he'd been dreading from her captain. She'd passed peacefully the night before in her cabin.

"Hey, you hack! I know you're there, 'cause ya ain't been off that tub in over a week." Baloney climbed aboard carrying a small box, an overnight letter envelope, and a six-pack of Red Stripe. He found a silent and subdued Sandy sitting on his aft deck. KC was across from him on his now vacant writing desk. The cat stood and mewed, obviously expecting to be petted by the newcomer. Baloney set his packages down and cautiously petted the cat.

"Hah! Must be tired of you bein' the only one to pet him. I guess we got a truce goin'."

"What do you want, Bill?"

That shook Baloney, whom Sandy had never called "Bill" before. "Well hello to you, too, you old hack. What do I want? Nothin'. I even brought my own beer, 'cause I knew you'd be 'fresh out.' Here." He handed Sandy a bottle.

"How did you know I'd want one?"

"'Cause the vultures ain't circling over this tub yet." Suddenly he looked sheepish, realizing what he'd said.

Sandy chuckled, "I'm too tough for them anyway." He leaned his bottleneck forward for Baloney to clink his against, which he did, happy to be forgiven for his thoughtless comment.

"Oh, hey, Barry the dockmaster asked me to drop these off for ya." He indicated the letter and the box. Both had the same return address of a law firm in Palm Beach.

Sandy opened the envelope and found the title to Betsy's center console outboard that had been transferred over to him. There was also a letter addressed to him. He decided to open it when he was alone.

He knew what was in the small box. Betty's ashes.

Baloney had been studying him. "You okay?"

"Yeah. As okay as I get these days."

"Well, I've been thinkin'. You've got all this extra time on yer hands now, and I've got a couple ah open dates comin' up, we maybe should go fishin' together. You just buy the fuel an' tip the mate. An' bring the beer, ah course."

Sandy knew the part about the open dates was a lie. Ever since he had become the star of *Tuna Hunters*, Baloney and his boat had been in high demand. He was moved by the offer and the sentiment behind it.

"That might have to be a plan. But meanwhile, I can't let you show up here with beer without me conning you out of it first. Just doesn't taste the same. What do you say we head over to the *Cove Beach Bar* and have a few, then we can argue about the tab."

"No argument from me, you can pay."

"That wasn't what I meant."

"I know." Baloney grinned and picked up the carrier with the remaining four beers.

"You can put the rest of them in that fridge." Sandy pointed to the one on the back deck.

"Uh, how 'bout no? We'll drop these off at my boat on the way."

"You brought those over here for me, to cheer me up... Gilligan!"

Baloney grinned, not even objecting to being called by that irritating nickname. "Yeah, mission accomplished. Ya still don't get ta keep the extras. Now c'mon, I hear those beach beers callin' that you're gonna buy me."

KC looked up at Sandy and smiled, happy to see his best food provider and pal looking happy again. Cats do know things.

A FEW DAYS LATER, Mimi, Sandy, Eric, Dawn, Casey, and Missy took Betsy's ashes out to the canyon where all but Mimi and Dawn had fished together with her. Sandy carefully opened the container and spread the gray, oatmeal-looking ash over the water. Then he looked at Missy and motioned to the helm.

"Take us home, kiddo."

She looked hesitant, "Are you sure?"

"Trust me, she'd have wanted you to. And don't spare the horsepower. They make new engines every day, and flat calm days like today are made for running flat out. Let's not waste this one." He smiled. The torch had been passed.

He pulled out the letter that had been in the overnight pouch and reread it for the umpteenth time:

SANDY, I hate that you're reading this letter, because I'd hoped we would have had a lot more time together. If the chemo had worked, you'd have never seen this, we'd have just let whatever we have going keep going the way it was. I know there would've been a lot of fishing, friends, and time for just the two of us as well. I'm sorry that didn't happen.

Thank you for showing me that there was life beyond grief and grieving, and still more left to do in this world. I wish I'd been able to follow through with it all with you but since I can't, I want you to.

As it is, if we can take one last ride together in my old boat, your new boat, I'll be forever grateful. Please bring Mimi and any of our fishing friends that would care to go. Take me to the spot where we caught all those tuna so when you fish those waters you'll always think of me. Please bring Missy along and take her under your wing. She's got the makings of a tournament champion. And for that last ride, give her some helm time on the way back in. No better day to start than today to pass the torch.

I'll leave you with this; remember what I told you that day in the pool: "Don't overthink things, Sandy, be a bit more impetuous and adventurous. Take a risk now and then." Live life, my friend, don't wait for adventure to come to find you. Grab it by the throat and shake all the fun out of it that you can. And if you meet someone special, say at a C2 party, don't hesitate to cast off and follow her a thousand miles if you have to. You won't regret it, trust me on this because I haven't regretted a second of it.

F*AIR WINDS AND FOLLOWING SEAS, my friend.*
   Betsy

H*E* LOOKED over at Casey and asked, "Hey, is that offer to go offshore kayak fishing with you still good..."

THE ADVENTURES of the gang from *Mallard Cove* continue in COASTAL JURY, Book #9 in the Coastal Adventure Series.

AUTHOR NOTES

Thanks so much for reading **Coastal Curse.** If you read this one before reading the first seven books in this series, **Coastal Conspiracy, Coastal Cousins, Coastal Paybacks, Coastal Tuna, Coastal Cats, Coastal Caper, and Coastal Culprit,** don't worry. While it's better if they are read in sequence, each can still be read as a "stand-alone" book with a minimum of "spoilers". I use the phrase *that's a story for another day* to refer to things that were covered more in-depth in those other volumes.

Hey, if you liked **Coastal Curse,** I'd appreciate it if you would kindly leave a review on Goodreads or Book Bub. Just a line or two would be great! And feel free to send me an email; I'd love to hear what you thought of this book. You can reach me at <u>contact@donrich-books.com.</u>

I also have a private **Reader's Group** where I share pictures and stories that inspired the books. You can sign up for the **Reader's Group** on my website, <u>http://www.donrichbooks.com</u>

If you're on Facebook, be sure to visit and "Like" my **Don Rich Books** page: <u>https://www.facebook.com/DonRichBooks/</u>

Thanks again!
Don Rich

GLOSSARY

I grew up on the water in South Florida and have an extensive boating background. I've worked on boats, built them, rebuilt them, and spent a good amount of time in boatyards. I've always loved boats, and ever since I was a pre-teenager, I haven't gone longer than six months without owning at least one. Most of my friends are boaters, too. So it's easy for me to forget that not everyone is as familiar with the jargon as my friends and me, which is something that I've now been reminded of on more than one occasion. (My apologies to those I ended up sending to the dictionary!) To make amends, here's a (growing) list of uniquely nautical terms and words that have been included in several of my books. Bear in mind that these definitions are based on my usage and experience. Things can be different from one region to another. For instance, you can fish for stripers in Montauk, New York, but here in Virginia, we fish for rockfish. But the true name for the target species is "striped bass."

So, here are the definitions of some of the more confusing words, at least as I know them. We'll start with a half dozen simple ones, then move on to those that are more complex:

- **Bow** the front of the boat.

- **Stern** back of the boat.
- **Port** the left side of the boat.
- **Starboard** the right side of the boat.
- **Aft** the rear of the boat.
- **Forward (fore)** the front of the boat.
- **Bow Thruster** a propeller in a tube that is mounted from side to side through the bow, allowing the captain more maneuverability and control when docking, especially in adverse winds and currents. Powered by an electric motor.
- **Bulkhead** boat wall.
- **Center Console** a type of boat with a raised helm console in the middle of the boat with space on each side to walk around. Most also incorporate a built-in bench seat or cooler seat in the front.
- **Chine** the longitudinal area running fore and aft where the bottom meets the side. It can be rounded or "sharp." They hurt when the boat rocks and it meets your head when you are swimming next to it. Trust me on that.
- **Circle Hook** a fishhook designed to get caught in the corner of a fish's mouth, keeping it from being ingested. Greatly reduces the mortality of fish that are released or that break the line.
- **Citation** at the airport, it's a type of jet made by Cessna. But here in Virginia, it's a slip of paper suitable for framing, issued by the state confirming that you caught a fish that's considered large for its particular species. Or it can be a speeding ticket, either on water or land. I like the fish kind better.
- **Covering Board** a flat surface at the top of a **gunwale** usually made out of teak or fiberglass, that's used as a step for boarding and for mounting recessed **rod holders**.
- **Deck** what floors on boats are called.
- **Fighting Chair** a specialized chair that can be turned to face a fish. Mounted on a sturdy stanchion with a built-in **gimbal**, the chair allows the angler to use the attached

footrest to use their legs and body to gain more leverage on a large fish. Most of today's fighting chairs are based on the design of my late friend John Rybovich.

- **Fish Box** a built-in storage box for the day's catch. They can be either elevated in the stern, or in the deck with a flush-mounted lid. On some of the higher-end sportfish boats, they can have a cooling system or an automatic icemaker that continually adds ice throughout the trip.
- **Fishing Cockpit** the lower aft deck on a sport fisherman that usually contains a **fighting chair, fish box,** and **tackle center.** Surrounded on three sides by the **gunwales** and the **stern.** The cockpit deck is usually just above the waterline, with **scuppers** that empty overboard. Can get flooded when backing down hard on a big fish.
- **Flying Bridge (Flybridge)** a permanently mounted helm area on top of the **wheelhouse.** Can be open or enclosed.
- **Following Sea** when the waves are moving toward the boat from behind the **stern.**
- **Gaff** a large barbless hook at the end of a pole, used for landing fish. They come in different sizes and lengths.
- **Gangway (Gangplank)** a removable ramp or set of stairs attached to the side of larger boats to allow easier access for boarding from a dock. Usually hinged to allow for tide variation.
- **Gear** marine transmission which has forward, neutral, and reverse.
- **Gin Pole** a vertical pole next to the gunwale usually rigged with a block and tackle and used for hauling large fish aboard. These used to be quite common until John Rybovich invented the **transom door** fifty years ago.
- **Gunwale** aft side area of a boat above the waterline, the area on either side of a fishing cockpit.
- **Hatch** a hole in a deck or bulkhead with a cover that may be hinged or completely removable. On a **sport**

fisherman, the door into the wheelhouse may be called either a **hatch** or a door.

- **Head** a bathroom, or a marine toilet.
- **Helm** the area that includes the steering and engine controls. In many sportfishing boats, the controls are mounted on a **helm pod**, a wood box with radiused edges that juts out of a cabinet or bulkhead.
- **Keys Conch** a person born in the Florida Keys. You can be born in Miami and move to the Keys an hour later and live there the rest of your life, and you will NEVER be a Conch. Usually, very tough, and independent characters.
- **Lean Seat** a high bench seat usually found behind the **helm** of a **center console**. Designed to be leaned against or sat upon. May have storage built-in under the seat section.
- **Mezzanine Deck** a shallow, raised deck on a sportfish just forward of the **fishing cockpit**, and aft of the **wheelhouse bulkhead**.
- **Outriggers** long aluminum poles on sportfishing boats that are raked up and aft from up alongside the wheelhouse. They are extended outward when fishing, having clips on lines that carry the fishing lines out away from the boat, creating a wider **spread**.
- **Pilot Boat** a smaller boat designed to handle all kinds of seas, whose sole purpose is delivering and retrieving a captain with extensive local knowledge to larger boats approaching or leaving a port.
- **Rod Holder** like the name suggests a device that a fishing rod butt is inserted into to hold it steady. There are recessed types that are mounted in **covering boards**, and exposed ones attached to railings or **tower** legs.
- **Salon** a living room area of a boat's cabin.
- **Scuppers** deck or cockpit drains.
- **SeaKeeper Gyro** a stabilizing gyro that almost eliminates roll in boats.

- **Shaft** attaches a **propeller** to the **gear**.
- **Sheer Line** the rail edge where the foredeck meets the side of the hull.
- **Sonar/Fish Finder** electronic underwater 'radar' that displays the sea floor, and anything between it and the boat.
- **Sportfisherman (Sportfish)** a unique style of boat designed specifically for fishing.
- **Spread** the arrangement of the baits being towed while trolling.
- **Stem** the forwardmost edge of the **bow**.
- **Stern** the farthest **aft** part of the boat, also called the **transom**.
- **Tackle Center** a cabinet in the **fishing cockpit** or the **center console** which holds hooks, swivels, leads, and other fishing supplies.
- **(Tuna) Tower** an aluminum pipe structure located above the **house** or the **flybridge** designed to hold spotters or riders, and may or may not have an additional **helm**.
- **Transom** stern.
- **Transom (Tuna) Door** a door in the stern just above the waterline, designed for boating large fish, but also useful for retrieving swimmers and divers.
- **Trough** the lowest point between waves.
- **Wheelhouse (House)** the cabin section of a boat which sometimes contains an enclosed helm.
- **Wheel (Steering)** controls the boat's direction.
- **Wheel (Propeller)** slang for the/a prop.

ABOUT THE AUTHOR

Don Rich is the author of the bestselling Coastal Adventure Series. Three of his books even simultaneously held the top three spots in Amazon's Hot New Releases in Boating.

Don's books are set mainly in the mid-Atlantic because of his love for this stretch of the Atlantic coastline. A fifth-generation Florida native who grew up on the water, he has spent a good portion of his life on, in, under, or beside it.

He now makes his home in central Virginia. When he's not writing or watching another fantastic mid-Atlantic sunset, he can often be found on the Chesapeake Bay or the Atlantic Ocean with a fishing rod in his hand.

MY "LATE" PALS

I owe a huge debt of thanks to my writer friends who "gave their all" in the "Stenny Boat." This came about on a private message board that we all use for, among other things, tossing around ideas for coastal stories. Four of them had just written a novella, Graceless, where a new fictional main character interacted with all of their own well-established main characters. Several of them had "borrowed" characters for cameos in their books in the past, but this was a completely new concept. The proceeds from Graceless will fund future advertising for TropicalAuthors.com (which I'll get into next).

This got me thinking, it would be fun to have a few of my writer pals become characters in **Coastal Curse**, and I could kill them off. (Ratings... it's all about the ratings...) I put it up on the message board, asking for volunteers, hoping to get two or even three if I was lucky. What happened next blew my mind. We hit three and they showed no hint of slowing down, eventually ending up with NINE-TEEN volunteers! I thought this is great! Wait, no, I realized that this is a disaster! I had planned on "taking out" the original two or three separately, but now everyone had to die at once to approach any semblance of realism. I know what you're thinking, that realism in a book with a voodoo mambo is a relative concept. But I do my best.

And THAT was how the "Stenny Boat" was born, which was named after my friend and fellow writer, Wayne Stinnett, who had an aversion to "giving his all" in this story, LOL!

So, I'd like to thank them all once again. Here's the list, in alphabetical order:

- Chip Bell
- David Berens
- Axel Blackwell
- Doug Brisotti
- John Cunningham
- Mac Fortner
- Evan Graver
- Jack Hardin
- Nicholas Harvey
- Kirk Jockell
- Steve Kittner
- Stewart Matthews
- Chris Niles
- Bryan Peabody
- Douglas Pratt
- Armand Rosamilia
- Jinx Schwartz
- Brian Spangler
- Nick Sullivan

I had originally planned to give my author pals more lines and "page time," but once the list got so long, I had to settle mostly for a little background information on each of them. Yes, it's all true, including the part about John Cunningham having been a Key West disco bouncer.

Once again, thank you all for volunteering. I hope it was painless...

THE TROPICAL AUTHORS

www.TropicalAuthors.com isn't fictional. In fact, as a fan of coastal stories, this is a fantastic tool for you to use to be able to find new coastal authors and a wide range of books within this genre. I'm proud to be an original member of the group, and so excited to have seen it grow into what it has become. We now have many thousands of coastal readers who rely on it each month. And it continues to grow and evolve, now having a twice-monthly newsletter announcing the latest releases, deals, and audiobooks in the coastal genre. A huge THANK YOU to its creator, Nick Sullivan, for adding me.

OCRACATS

Rita and Ocracats are both real. Their mission is real as well. I'm a HUGE fan, and three of our "fur kids" are Ocracats including Casey Shaw, who "KC" in this story is based upon. Though the story of Blackbeard's cats (Chester and Anne) is purely fiction... or, is it?

You can learn more about this organization at www.ocracats.org including how you can help, and how you can register to adopt a kitten and give one a loving, forever home.

ALSO BY DON RICH

Check my website www.DonRichBooks.com for the current list of all my book titles.

The Coastal Beginnings Series:

(The prelude to the Coastal Adventure Series)

- COASTAL CHANGES
- COASTAL TREASURE
- COASTAL RULES
- COASTAL BLUFFS

The Coastal Adventure Series:

- COASTAL CONSPIRACY
- COASTAL COUSINS
- COASTAL PAYBACKS
- COASTAL TUNA
- COASTAL CATS
- COASTAL CAPER
- COASTAL CULPRIT
- COASTAL CURSE
- COASTAL JURY
- COASTAL CURRENCY
- COASTAL CRUISE

Other Books by Don Rich:

- GhostWRITER

Here's A Tropical Authors Novella by Deborah Brown, Nicholas Harvey, and Don Rich:

- **Priceless**

Go to my website at www.DonRichBooks.com for more information about joining my **Reader's Group**! And you can follow me on Facebook at: https://www.facebook.com/DonRichBooks

I'm also a member of TropicalAuthors.com, where you can find my latest books and those by dozens of my coastal writer friends!

9 781959 126348